Alton Clyde

# Tried and True

SALZWASSER
VERLAG

**Alton Clyde**

# Tried and True

Reprint of the original, first published in 1863.

1st Edition 2022 | ISBN: 978-3-37500-337-1

Verlag (Publisher): Salzwasser Verlag GmbH, Zeilweg 44, 60439 Frankfurt, Deutschland
Vertretungsberechtigt (Authorized to represent): E. Roepke, Zeilweg 44, 60439 Frankfurt, Deutschland
Druck (Print): Books on Demand GmbH, In de Tarpen 42, 22848 Norderstedt, Deutschland

# TRIED AND TRUE.

## A TALE.

BY ALTON CLYDE.

Creatures not too pure or good,
For human nature's daily food;
For transient sorrows, simple wiles,
Praise, blame, love, kisses, tears, and smiles.

WORDSWORTH.

London

1868.

# TRIED AND TRUE.

---

## CHAPTER I.

"HAVE you nothing to give me, Grace? I am so faint and weary, and I think if I could only eat, I should soon get strong. Have you nothing for me, Grace?" And the sick man turned feebly on his pillow, extended his worn hand over the scanty coverlet, and looked with almost pitiful eagerness towards a slight young girl who sat close to the window, making the most of the waning daylight, and stitching as if the chances of life and death were hanging on every frail thread.

A spasm of anguish crossed the care-worn young face as she hurriedly answered, still sewing on, for she could not afford to lose one moment of the precious light,

"I have nothing yet, father, that you can eat, only the dry toast and gruel."

The invalid turned away his face with a fretful wailing moan that went to the heart of the pale worker. The dusky evening shadows were darkening over the room, which was one of the most ill-ventilated and ill-furnished that could have been found even in that class of London lodging-houses. The gas lamps were lighted in the court when Grace Arnold rose from her seat, and with flushed cheeks and brightening eyes held up for final inspection the dress to which she had just put the finishing touch. Then she went to her father's bedside, and bent over him, whispering tenderly, "I have finished my work, father; only keep up your heart, and you shall have something to make you strong. The doctor said you ought to have wine, and you shall have it"—If I sit up every night, she was going to add, but she checked the words on her lips, and busied herself with arranging the bed clothes.

"Grace, are you going out?" asked the sick man, raising himself on his pillow with painful effort.

"Yes, father, to take home my work."

"You will not be long gone?"

"Oh, no, dear father," she answered, cheerfully; "and when I come back, I mean to make you such a nice tempting supper."

"You are a good girl, Grace, you always were." He laid his hand caressingly on hers and looked at her with dim eyes, all the querulous selfishness of sickness being for the time forgotten in the stirring of nobler feelings. He was touched by the devotion with which his only child had clung to him in all the chances and changes of his fortune. Mr. Arnold had not always occupied his present position, and Grace had not always toiled for daily bread. She could look back to a home where a fond mother smiled upon her, and they had all the comforts and refinements of life. To use a common but most expressive phrase, the Arnolds had seen better days. It is needless to go further into a painful history; such vicissitudes are of every day occurrence — the inevitable consequence of the commercial failures that are continually agitating the money-making world. The poor father's heart might well yearn with tenderness towards his daughter, for nothing had outlived his prosperity except her love.

"You are wearing yourself out, my poor Grace. You must take better care of yourself, child, or Harry will not know you when he comes home."

At these last words there was a start, a vivid blush, and a sudden brightness in her eyes. The life of the poor dressmaker had its under current of love and happiness, which once in every life-time comes as natural to the young heart as the morning gush of song to the sky-lark.

"Who is that dress for, Grace?"

"Mrs. Foster."

The sick man sank back with a sigh of disappointment. "The lady who owes you so much, love? Perhaps she will not even pay you for this."

"Oh, yes, father," said Grace, putting on her faded black bonnet with trembling haste, "she cannot refuse when she knows we are in such need, and that it has taken all the money I had to buy the trimmings. Oh, no, she cannot surely refuse."

* * * *

## CHAPTER II.

"AH! there is the dressmaker with my new brocade, Alice, love. I wish you would just go and speak to the young person, for I really don't feel quite equal to the exertion just now."

"Dear me, ma, how very provoking, just when I was practising this difficult air."

And the young lady rose from the piano with a very unwilling grace.

"It will not detain you long, my dear; I never like to keep poor people waiting, for to them time is money. And, now I think of it, Alice, she had better take back with her your new French merino, you can give your own instructions about the style of trimmings; and, my dear, be sure you impress upon her that the dress must be brought home by Friday evening at the latest. Now I know many ladies," Mrs. Foster continued, complacently settling herself in her easy chair, as her daughter swept out of the room, "who would not think of employing a dressmaker of that class; but I am above such prejudices. Wherever I meet talent of any kind, however humble its position, I like to encourage it and bring it forward. This is a superior sort of young person, and her work is done quite as well as it would be even in one of the first-class establishments, and—"

"So much cheaper," added a voice from the further end of the room, abruptly finishing the sentence.

The bold speaker was a niece of Mrs. Foster's, then staying with her on a visit. A little, slight thing, with very bright black eyes. She had not spoken a word for some time, but had been sitting in a distant corner with her face nearly eclipsed behind the leaves of a huge folio which she seemed to have been intently studying.

Mrs. Foster's cheek flushed angrily. But as it chanced that this young lady was a wealthy heiress, and she was anxious to make up a match between her and her eldest son, she could not afford to be offended. It was against her line of policy.

Mrs. Foster was a prudent woman; she instantly smoothed her ruffled feathers, and replied, with a short, forced laugh,

"You little book-worm, what could put such an idea into your head. I really don't know where you get all your odd sayings; but it is impossible to be displeased with you, so you take an unfair advantage. Fanny dear, I wish you would not sit so far away from the fire; it looks so unsocial, my love."

"Do you think so, aunt?" said the uncompromising heiress, giving her a shrewd look out of the corners of her black eyes.

She did not change her seat, but went on reading, leaving Mrs. Foster to draw her own conclusions.

In the meantime, a somewhat different scene was passing in another room of the same well-appointed mansion. On one side of a table heaped with elegant trifles, stood the only daughter of the house of Foster, stately, fair, and well-dressed, lightly resting her white, ringed hand on a parcel, about which she was condescendingly giving directions to poor Grace Arnold, who stood shrinking back, as if painfully conscious of all that separated them. With her young face prematurely sharpened, flushed, anxious, and trembling, she stood, while the hope that had sustained her was fast ebbing away; tightly crushing her small hands together, as if to choke back some involuntary expression of suffering which she feared might be forced from her, revealing all the home misery.

Here were two great social contrasts;

Dress-wearer and Dress-maker. The picture was a study in itself.

"I—I hope you will not be displeased, Miss Foster," poor Grace faltered out at last, when the young lady, who seemed to have a decided talent for business, had run through a string of minute directions concerning the quality and style of the trimmings to be purchased for her new dress, "but I wish to speak to your mamma for a moment," Grace continued, making a painful effort to approach the question which, since her father's illness, had become one of such vital importance to her, remuneration for her labour. "If I could only see Mrs. Foster for one moment!" she went on, nervously twitching a corner of her shawl, while her cheek flushed in painful confusion, and her eyes sought the carpet, more like a culprit detected in a fraud than one who was only asking her just right.

The young lady elevated her eyebrows in disdainful surprise, she considered the dressmaker's manner quite incomprehensible.

"You appear to have forgotten that I told you mamma was engaged this evening, Miss Arnold? Is your business really so important that another time will not do as well?"

Poor Grace! The vision of her home rose up before her, with its cheerless hearth so bare of warmth and comfort. Her sick father lying pale and helpless, with his pitiful cry wailing in her ear, "Have you nothing to give me, Grace?" and as a background to this picture there was the landlord fiercely clamouring for arrears of rent, and a crowd of small creditors rudely reproaching her with broken promises of payment. Truly her business was important.

"Oh! if they knew all; if I could only tell them," murmured the poor girl to herself, as she thrust back the hot tears that filled her eyes.

"Perhaps you would like to leave a message for mamma?" said Miss Foster, becoming slightly impatient.

"Oh, yes!" said Grace, eagerly catching at this forlorn hope.

Briefly and timidly she then told the history of her embarrassment, concluding with her modest request for a small payment upon the old account.

"I will deliver your message, but I cannot say how mamma will receive it. She is not accustomed to be urged in this way by the people whom she employs. You may wait a few moments," and without deigning to notice the effect of her words, proud Alice Foster swept out of the room, compressing the ample folds of her silk dress as she passed Grace that it might not come in contact with the dressmaker's rusty mourning. It was only a slight action, but it was strongly characteristic.

The next few minutes was an age of suspense and anxiety to Grace. Until now she had always shrank from making any appeal to Mrs. Foster's tardy sense of justice, for that lady was one of her principal employers, and she feared (not without reason) that such a course would involve the loss of her patronage. Alone, sickening for want of food, for dinner had been a fiction to the poor dressmaker that day, the interval of suspense was becoming almost beyond endurance, when a pert page, who looked as if he had outgrown his livery, entered, and with an insolent stare handed her a note from his mistress.

It contained only a few words, to the effect that Mrs. Foster's engagements made it impossible for her to attend to Miss Arnold's business that evening, but if she would call about eleven o'clock on Thursday morning she would probably be at leisure to look over her account. The note expressed some stately surprise at the nature of the message which Miss Foster had delivered, and concluded with a pointed request that Miss Arnold would not trouble herself to take with her the French merino dress, as it was not particularly wanted, and had only been offered from a charitable wish to keep her employed.

Grace uttered no exclamation as she finished reading the note. She was to all appearance perfectly calm, but her young brow was furrowed into unnatural lines, her shoulders had a weary stoop, and her slight figure bent as under some crushing weight, and her tearless eyes had a dull fixed look. If Mrs. Foster could have seen her then, she would surely have been moved to some womanly show of pity.

It was a sad picture of dejected hopelessness: as if the pulses of life were deadened, and she had not vitality left to grasp any keen sense even of her own miseries. She unconsciously dropped the note, which was suffered to lie unheeded where it fell. She did not recollect it until some time after, when it was beyond her power to recover it, and the pert page had closed the hall door upon her, as she shrunk away, faint and heart sick, from the sight of the crimson curtained windows that were sending forth a ruddy glow of light into the chill November dusk.

## CHAPTER III.

Poor Grace was toiling up the last flight of steep dark stairs, for the room they occupied was on the third floor. Her step was lingering and slow, for her heart was heavy, and she was trying to think of some way by which she could soften for her father the bitterness of the disappointment which seemed to have crushed the last hope out of her heart. If she had had none but herself to care for in that hour, she might have sunk down in the spiritless apathy of despair and let the dark waves of fate close over her head. She was saved by the blessed necessity that obliged her to think for another, and the oft-recurring thought that there was one whom she loved dependent on her care for everything on this side the grave.

"No, I must hide the worst from him. Whatever happens, he must be kept hopeful. We can afford to lose anything but hope: it is such a precious thing."

As Grace murmured these words her step grew lighter. It was at this moment that she felt a gentle pull at the skirt of her dress, and "It's only me, miss," came in a smothered whisper from a small treble voice as she started and turned round. It was the poor little hard-worked drudge of the house, whose entire existence was bounded by the scrubbing brush, and who might be said, literally as well as figuratively, to be always living in hot water, for the anger of her mistress was continually descending on her devoted head.

There was a curious bond of sympathy between Grace and this little forlorn being. It was simply the working of the Divine law of kindness. Grace was perhaps the only one who ever spoke gently to the poor child or treated her with any consideration, and she had several times saved her from unjust punishment. Poor Susan almost worshipped the young dressmaker. She did not know how to express it, but still she had a feeling of her own that Grace, with her pale face, her little white hands, and her soft voice, belonged to an order of beings very far above the people among whom she now lived.

If Grace had been less sad at heart she might have been inclined to laugh at the picture before her. Divided between her fear of being detected, and her eagerness to arrest Grace's attention, the little maid of all work had lost one of her old slippers on the stairs, and her distress at this circumstance was ludicrously mingled with other feelings. She brought with her a warm damp odour of soap and wet clothes, for washing was going on in the remote lower regions.

"What is the matter, Susan? I hope you

have not been getting into more trouble," said Grace, in her sweet grave voice, as she paused on the stairs, looking at the poor little creature in kind pity.

"No, miss, nothing to speak of," Susan replied, thrusting her red knuckles into her eyes at this allusion to her own private griefs; "I only just waited to know if you has any errands to do, for I be a-going out soon to fetch beer for the back parlour. And please, Miss Grace, there's a man brought a letter for your father. Missis told me to take it up, as the man said it was to be give in his own hands. And please," continued the girl, apologetically, "I lit the candle, and stirred the fire, cause I thought he'd like it."

"Thank you, Susan, that was very thoughtful and kind. No, I think I shall not want you to night, Susan; take care you do not fall, the stairs are very dark."

And Grace went wearily up to her own room, unconscious how her gentle words were treasured in the forlorn heart that was always hungering for a little kindness, or how a friendless human life was made brighter and happier through her means.

"Grace, Grace," said the sick man's wailing, querulous voice, "is it you at last? I thought you would never come, child." She found her father sitting up in bed with an open letter in his shaking hands which he was vainly trying to read by the dim light of the unsnuffed candle. His breath came quick and hard, his cheeks burned with unwonted fire, and there was a restless, excited glitter in his eyes. The daughter's heart sank in vague, terrified foreboding.

"Come here, Grace, and read this; read, read, for yourself. I cannot make it out clearly by this light," and the letter was impatiently thrust towards her. She took it with a sickening sense of dread, of she knew not what. As she prepared to read, her father fastened his dry, glittering eyes on her face, and tightened his clasp upon the coverlet till the veins started out from the back of his white hand, like knots of dim purple cords.

It was not long before Grace understood, only too well, the cause of her father's agitation. The letter came from the wealthy uncle of Harry Clare, the young man to whom Grace had plighted her faith in days of happiness and prosperity. This uncle was the great man of the Clare family. As he had no children, he adopted Harry in his boyhood, and had him educated as the future heir of his wealth; but beyond the ties of relationship and gratitude, the uncle and nephew were not drawn together by any dearer feeling, for nothing could be more dissimilar than the natures of the cold, calculating man of the world and the generous high-spirited youth who had won Grace Arnold's early love. At the time of their engagement, the elder Clare had not shown himself much opposed to it; but since Mr. Arnold's reverse of fortune he had formed other views for his nephew. It was in order to see if separation and absence would effect what he had vainly tried, the estrangement of the young pair, that he contrived to be in sudden and serious perplexity for want of a trustworthy agent to transact some important business for him at Calcutta, and so successfully worked upon Harry's sense of duty that the young man, without any suspicion of his uncle's real intentions, consented to undertake the mission, making it a condition that on his return he and Grace were to be married.

"Well, well, my boy," the uncle had answered evasively, "if you both remain in the same mind we shall see; young folks are not to be trusted. Go and see a little of the world first."

The letter announced that Harry Clare was now on his way home, and as his uncle had gathered from the tone of his letters that he was not yet cured of his passion for Grace Arnold, he had resolved to take more effectual means to separate the lovers. His plans were soon formed. He had a promissory note from Mr. Arnold for the repayment of a certain sum of money which he had advanced to him in his necessities. This was the instrument of power which he now determined to use over the unfortunate gentleman whom he had once called his friend, though he knew to what abject poverty his unhappy debtor was reduced, and that he was stretched on a sick bed, from which even his daughter despaired to see him ever rise. He urged what he knew was impossible in their present circumstances, the immediate repayment of the money, or at least of a part; and scrupled not to arm himself with the terrors of the law, and threaten the man whom he knew to be slowly dying in that miserable attic with the last crushing calamity of a debtor's prison.

The only condition on which his forbearance could be purchased was through Grace. He offered to forego his claim on her father, and even hinted at the possibility of a further advance, if she would consent to break off her engagement with his nephew, and give him her written promise that she would never encourage any future addresses from Harry Clare. It was a heartless, cruel letter, one that only such a man could have written.

Grace read it to the end with white, quivering lips, a wildly-beating heart, and throbbing brain.

"And this comes from a Clare," said the sick man with a painful catch of his breath. "It almost makes me hate the name. Grace, Grace, what is to be done?"

"There is no choice left, father. We are in his power, and must purchase forbearance at his own hard price."

"What, Grace, would you let him wring such a pledge from you?"

"Oh, father, can you doubt me. Do you think I would let them drag you to prison while it is in my power to save you? I would sign away my own life rather than see you come to such a fate;" and Grace crept shudderingly towards the bed, and almost wildly kissed one of his wasted hands.

"My noble, precious child, I have done nothing to deserve this."

"It is my duty, dear father, and I will not shrink from it."

"No, Grace," said Mr. Arnold firmly, the last feeble, flickering spark of physical strength flaming up with unnatural vigour, "it would be sin to suffer such a sacrifice. I feel that my life is drawing to an end, and it will make but little difference whether I close my eyes in a prison or in this room. Let old Matthew Clare do what he threatens; his persecution can extend no further, and the disgrace will remain with him. Poverty is not a crime."

But Grace was still unshaken in her generous resolution.

"It must be, father; sooner or later it would come to this. I should have to give up Harry, for his uncle would never consent to our marriage, and you know that Harry's future prospects are all dependent upon him, and I would not be the means of bringing discord into a family. No, father, Harry and I must part, our ways in life are so different now."

Grace spoke firmly, though she had to stifle many a heaving sob in the effort, and her beautiful brown eyes were dim with unshed tears:

Mr. Arnold pondered a moment, then his eyes brightened suddenly, and he said,

"Grace, I have only just thought of it. The money that Mrs. Foster owes you will be just enough to satisfy a part of Mr. Clare's demand. If we can only pay him, and save you from being bound by a hateful pledge, it will be a satisfaction to me before I die. Never mind me, Grace, I can do without wine, anything, so that we may be free from that man."

Grace read in her father's look the inquiry she had been dreading, about the result of her errand to Mrs. Foster's. She thought it best to anticipate his questions, so she said soothingly,

"I took home my work father, but Mrs. Foster was engaged and could not see me. I am to go to her on Thursday morning."

Mr. Arnold uttered a fretful, weary sigh. She went on,

"This delay has troubled me a good deal, father, for your sake. It was a cruel disappointment, but ladies like Mrs. Foster do not comprehend our necessities, they know nothing of us; we are out of reach of their sympathies, and they cannot understand how a trifle of money is sometimes a question of life or death to us."

Grace had unconsciously spoken some stern truths. Her words would have sounded bitter if they had not been softened by her gentle voice.

Her father did not answer. Within the last few moments there was a change in him that alarmed her. A glazed film crept over his eyes, and his hands relaxed their hold of the bed clothes. Exhausted, and almost fainting, he sank back on his pillows with a low moan.

His false strength was fast ebbing away. This was the reaction which Grace had feared, the excitement of the last half-hour had already told upon his feeble frame. The shock of the letter had visibly shaken the lessening sands in his hour-glass. Grace tenderly wiped the cold dews from his forehead, and moistened his pale lips with a little cordial which had been providentially left in one of the bottles. After which, seeing him somewhat revived, she set herself resolutely to work to renew the expiring fire and prepare him a cup of tea, in the purchase of which she had that evening expended her last few pence; bustling about to give the room the nearest approach to an air of comfort that it was capable of receiving. When their scanty meal was over, and her father, seemingly more refreshed and composed, had sunk into a slumber that relieved her anxious watch by his bed-side, Grace stole into the little closet that by a stretch of courtesy was called her bed-room. Perhaps the full heart could only there give free vent to its pent-up agony.

When she came out, her eyes looked as if she had been weeping. There were dark purple lines under their drooping lashes, and her white, worn face had a hopeless, despairing look. She was very quiet and calm, but her resolution was taken. She would never allow her father to suspect what it would cost her to renounce the love, dearer than life, which had grown with her growth, and strengthened with her strength. Grace was not one of those noisy, demonstrative persons whose deepest feelings always lie upon the surface. Perhaps it was a merciful dispensation that the stern, practical duties of life left her no time to sentimentalize and nurse her own sorrows in selfish exclusion of all other claims. The fire of adversity had tried and purified the gold of her nature. Good, conscientious Grace, it was like herself to sit down, as she did, and begin bravely stitching at the homely stuff dress which her landlady had benevolently given her to make that it might help to pay off their arrears of rent; it was characteristic of the self-forgetfulness and enduring patience that formed the underlying strength of her character. Grace Arnold, in that squalid room, in the midst of such surroundings, with her pure, pale beauty, gentle, lady-like manners, refined instincts, and delicate tastes, was like one of those sweet wild flowers, that we may sometimes see blooming in some hidden out-of-the-way nook where we least expected to find such treasures, nestling at the foot of a rugged craig, or gleaming out like stars under the brow of some dark, frowning rock, breathing away their fragrant lives in rough desert places; all the more beautiful for the barrenness that surrounds them, and filling their appointed place, with sweet content, from which restless, human ambition would do well to take a lesson.

The following day confirmed all the anxious daughter's secret fears about her father, who had become all the dearer to her for the sake of his misfortunes, his illness, and helpless dependence upon herself. He was alarmingly worse. The dread reality could no longer be disguised in those delusive hopes which blind the fond credulity of affection until the flattering self-deception becomes impossible. Poor Grace felt that she would soon be alone in the world, and in the heart-sickness that came with the thought, she realized, even then, all the sense of desolation conveyed in those few words. But the two great lessons of her life had been endurance and self-restraint. Hers was that rare refinement of human love that seeks not its own but the happiness of the beloved. So the dear, brave girl went on doing her duty calmly and self-collectedly, without any ostentatious parade of her own feelings. Always trying, for her father's sake, to keep the grieved look out of her sad eyes, that would steal over her face when she was alone.

Mr. Arnold showed a strange, troubled

restlessness about his daughter. He would scarcely suffer her to leave him, and watched her about the room with a wistful solicitude that she well understood. As his physical strength failed his sensibilities seemed to quicken, and his perceptions grew clearer. The letter from Matthew Clare was still agitating his mind. He often drew his daughter's hand in his, and smoothed her hair, an old familiar action to which she had been used from childhood.

"Grace," he spoke with difficulty, as if collecting all his strength into the effort, "You must not write to that man, or sign any promise to him. I could not die happy if I thought you had so bound yourself. Let Harry decide it. If he is willing to give you up to secure worldly gain for himself he does not deserve my darling."

The fear of old Matthew Clare constantly haunted poor Grace. She lived in hourly dread of seeing her father prostrated by another blow from the same cruel hand. She feared to leave him even for a few minutes, and if Susan came to tell her that she was wanted down stairs, the message would throw her into an agony of trepidation. In addition to this she had other cruel anxieties. These were the every-day necessities of life which she had no means to satisfy, and all the terrors of impending destitution which her days and nights of exhausting toil had failed to ward off. Her sick father engrossed all her time and care, for he required her almost constantly at his bedside. The doctor called sometimes; a brusque, coarse man, who was always in bustling haste, and whose loud voice and portly figure seemed to over-fill the little room. He shook his head oracularly when the pale girl privately questioned him about her father's condition, and prescribed various expensive delicacies for the patient, while poor Grace had not money to procure another loaf of bread; and he might have read in her sad young face all the tale of privation which her proud sensitive heart shrank from revealing.

In spite of all former disappointments, the interview with Mrs. Foster on Thursday morning was poor Grace's sole anchor of hope now. But how were they to live in the meantime? She had nothing that could be converted into money, not even a trinket; the wreck had spared nothing. And they had not a relative or friend in the wide world of whom they could claim assistance. For a moment Grace yearned towards him whom she had looked upon as her future husband, but only for a moment. The thought was sternly and resolutely thrust aside. What must be done? She returned again and again to this question, but always with the same hopeless result. It was enough to make even her brave heart sink in despair.

Mr. Arnold became worse towards evening. His cough was not so violent, but he was visibly weaker. His voice failed him, and his breathing became short and difficult, but still his dim eyes followed his daughter with the old wistful anxiety.

At last Grace formed a bold resolution. To write to her wealthy employer, Mrs. Foster. Write to her that night, and tell her the truth, that her father was dying, dying in want. With a Christian and a woman such an appeal could not fail.

When the sick man had sunk into one of the restless slumbers that left him so little refreshed, Grace seized the opportunity for which she had been waiting, and lighting the solitary candle, withdrew into her own little room, fearing that the light might awake the sleeper. The letter was soon written and folded. It contained only a few earnest words, but the heart of the writer bled in them. It was the simple natural utterance of great sorrow. It took only a few minutes to steal down-stairs and get the landlady's ready consent for Susan to take the letter to Mrs. Foster's, with instructions to wait for an answer. Then the small servant departed on her mission at her utmost speed, full of pleased importance to think she could be of use to Miss Grace, for whose sake she would have cheerfully undertaken a pilgrimage in any kind of weather to the furthest corner of the great city.

## CHAPTER IV.

Mrs. Foster's pert page in the tight fitting livery, who had answered Susan's timid ring, stood holding the hall door in his hand and looking unutterable things at the dressmaker's odd-looking but most zealous messenger.

"You don't mean to say it's you that's been a-ringing our bell," said the fast specimen of pageship, with an incredulous sniff, twirling his thumb in a manner that was meant to be impressively facetious, and peering insolently under the flapping brim of the overgrown black bonnet, which had descended to little Susan from an old maiden aunt of her mistress's, in which her face looked as if buried under a huge extinguisher.

"I've brought this letter for the lady who lives here," panted Susan, who had scarcely yet recovered from the long hurried walk which, at every few yards of her progress, had expanded into a run, in her eagerness to do Grace's errand with all possible speed, for she was shrewd enough to guess that it was of importance; "and please, sir, Miss Grace said I was to wait," she added, apprehensively. Profoundly awed by the grand look of the house, and fearfully impressed by the manner of the page, the poor child fixed her eyes in a sort of fascination on the last of the row of bright buttons adorning that young gentleman's coat. Higher than this she did not attempt to raise her eyes.

"For our Missis? Well, I'm blest if this ain't good fun. Some begging letter, I know; but that dodge won't take here, so you had better take yourself off, short-un."

"Oh, please! you must give her the letter,"

pleaded Susan. "It's from Miss Grace, who makes the lady's dresses; she said I was to be sure and wait."

The virtuous indignation of the page seemed to be satisfied with this explanation. Perhaps he was gratified by the evident awe, with which he had inspired the poor little servant. It was something quite novel to find any one afraid of him—or we will hope that it was some latent impulse of human feeling that made him say:—

"Why you look ready to cry; come, hand it over, and you may come in, and wait while I take it up."

He took the note, and glanced curiously at the delicate writing on the cover, which would not have disgraced Miss Foster herself. Then closed the hall door, and left poor Susan standing on one of the mats, quite oppressed with the stately air of the house, in which she scarcely dared to breath.

° ° ° °

Mrs. Foster and her daughter had just finished the all-important business of dressing for an evening party, which was expected to be one of the gayest assemblies of the season. It wanted scarcely ten minutes to the hour for which they had ordered the carriage, and John was always punctual.

The fair Alice was giving herself a last critical survey in the glass, and her mother was watching her, with a smile of gratified pride.

"Mamma," said the conscious beauty, with a slight curl of her full red lip; "what an unaccountable creature cousin Fanny is; I shall really pity our poor George, if he does succeed in catching this heiress. What a stupid whim to stay away from a party for no other earthly reason than to pore over stupid books. I protest she is quite a blue stocking. That outlandish Indian uncle has spoiled her, she has no proper pride. It is a shame that such a fine fortune should be thrown away on one so unworthy of it."

And sighing over this unfair adjustment of things, the speaker looked again at the lovely vision in the glass. She knew well that her father lived to the height of his income, that with five sons to provide for and settle in life, it would be out of his power to bestow any dowry upon his daughter. Young as she was, Alice Foster knew the full meaning of marrying for an establishment.

At this rather inauspicious moment there was a short quick rap at the dressing-room door, almost immediately followed by the apparition of the young heiress, Fanny Templeton, the unconscious subject of Miss Foster's cousinly censures.

Both ladies invited her in with much show of amiable feeling, and Mrs. Foster called her a dear, naughty, wilful girl for disappointing them so cruelly about the party, declaring that her absence would spoil all their evening's pleasure. But the sceptical young lady always seemed to take a perverse and undutiful delight in tripping up her aunt's flourishing speeches. She now cut her short by presenting Grace Arnold's note, which she had just received from the sagacious page, who was not disposed to risk the anger of his mistress by disturbing her at such a time.

Mrs. Foster looked puzzled and annoyed as she took the note, and Fanny said, with a provoking gleam of demure mischief in her black eyes:

"I believe it is from your late protegé, aunt; the young dressmaker whose abilities you extolled so warmly the day she brought home your new brocade. Pedro says that a little girl came with the note; she is now waiting for an answer."

Pedro was the title which the page had received from Mrs. Foster in exchange for his own humbler name of Peter, which did not please the ears of his lady.

"How very annoying," said Alice, turning from the glass with an angrily flushing cheek. "The impertinence of that young person is beyond everything. But you know I warned you, mamma, against employing such people."

"Very extraordinary, indeed!" commented Mrs. Foster, putting up her gold eye glass to glance over the words which poor Grace had written in such anguish. "It appears that she is in distress, something about her father being ill. But the writing is so pale I cannot make it out. I will look over her account to-morrow;" and Mrs. Foster coolly handed the note to her daughter.

"It is always the way with these people, they can always get up a tale of distress when they have a purpose to gain. I thought her an artful girl from the first. But hark! there is the carriage. It is impossible to attend to this to-night;" and Alice impatiently drew on her white kid gloves, without bestowing any further notice on Grace's note, which was left carelessly lying amidst the confusion of the toilet table.

With a cold laconic good-night to each,

Fanny Templeton darted off to her own room, and the two ladies swept down stairs, the younger murmuring to herself, as she looked after her cousin: "Odious creature! I wish her visit here was at an end."

As the ladies swept through the hall, poor wondering Susan held her breath, and crushed herself painfully into a corner until the dazzling vision had passed.

The carriage that bore away her aunt and cousin was scarcely out of hearing when Fanny Templeton went back to the deserted dressing-room. Full of the benevolent purpose which she had just formed, with her usual impulsiveness, she possessed herself of the neglected note. At first there was some little hesitation. She looked at it irresolutely, but her scruples of conscience were soon silenced, Fanny was a clever adept at finding cogent, substantial reasons to justify anything she wished to do.

"There can be no breach of confidence here," she whispered to herself. "This note was left open on the dressing table, at the mercy of the first servant who might chance to enter the room, I shall not possess myself of its contents in any covert, dishonourable way, for I mean to tell Aunt Foster all about it."

To read the note, was but the work of a moment. How it moved the impulsive, excitable Fanny, was revealed in each expressive line of her dark, handsome face, in which every change of thought and feeling was reflected as in a mirror. Her large black eyes were full of indignant tears, which flashed like sparks of fire under their long, dusky fringes.

"And my aunt professed to be a friend to this poor girl. Oh, it is too heartless! To hold a human life so cheaply, and talk coldly of to-morrow, as if it was merely a matter of business. When Aunt Foster loses at cards, to odious old Mrs. Martin, who is rich as a jewess, she will make any sacrifice rather than leave the debt unpaid. That, I suppose, is a debt of honour. But this, to the poor dressmaker, is considered quite a different thing. I call it robbery, and robbery of the basest kind, this defrauding of the poor out of their labour. But something must be done. Ah, now I recollect. Pedro said there was a girl waiting for an answer." Fanny Templeton delivered these thoughts in her own vehement characteristic way. With her, to resolve was to act. She went down stairs at once, and astonished Pedro, and two giggling housemaids, who were trying to extract some amusement out of poor Susan, by taking the bewildered little servant under her powerful wing, and sweeping her off to the back drawing room—the same room in which Grace had received Mrs. Foster's note.

Not allowing Susan much time to collect her scattered thoughts, she drew from her as much of Grace Arnold's history as the little servant could tell. How good she had always been to her sick father, how she worked and pinched herself for him, and how sweet and kind she was to everybody.

These were the staple facts of Susan's narration. The blundering grammar, and the seemingly hopeless mass of broken sentences and disjointed words, might have puzzled any other listener. But Fanny was satisfied. She was too warmly interested to care for these defects. Her own vivid imagination could fill up the outlines and supply all the details which were wanting.

"I must see her to-night," murmured Fanny, drawing out her purse, and opening it with eager, trembling fingers; "I will get dear old Morris to go with me, and this girl can be our guide. This is the first time that I ever really rejoiced in being dear Uncle Brian's heiress." She turned to Susan, saying aloud, "Wait here, until I return to you, and remember this is for yourself," and she pressed a half-crown into the girl's hand.

Susan's round eyes dilated to their widest

extent, and her mouth opened with some vague purpose of thanking the lady, but nothing came of it. A half-crown was to her an incredible mine of wealth, for her imagination in its wildest flights had never soared above a humble shilling. No wonder that her simple mind was almost overpowered by this sudden acquisition of riches.

Fanny Templeton had too nice a sense of the ridiculous, and too keen an appetite for its enjoyment, to be able to resist the temptation of being excessively amused by the ludicrous affect of her generosity on the little servant. "Oh, how I should like to take a sketch of her in that attitude," she whispered to herself, puckering up the corners of her mouth in the effort to look grave. But at this moment the recollection of Grace Arnold and her dying father rebuked the jest on her lips, and bitterly reproaching herself for her want of feeling, she hurriedly left the room, saying "I must go and find Morris. I can do nothing without her help."

Morris, upon whom the impetuous, self-willed heiress seemed to place such reliance, was a kind motherly-looking elderly woman, who had been the attached personal attendant of Fanny's mother, before her marriage to Mr. Templeton. She had been the young lady's earliest nurse, and was now promoted to the more dignified post of housekeeper. She dearly loved the young orphan, and would not yield to anyone the privilege of superintending her wardrobe, and waiting upon her. She always accompanied Miss Templeton on her travels, was the repository of all her little feminine secrets, and could influence the capricious, high-spirited girl, to an extent that often during the present visit had excited the jealous envy of the scheming, match-making aunt, who had vainly tried all her art to estrange the heiress from her faithful friend.

Fanny found the good creature in her own dressing room, busy as she left her, darning an almost imperceptible rent in a lace scarf;

for her recklessness always furnished plenty of work for Morris's skilful needle.

Another moment, and the work was all swept aside.

In this, as in other things, Fanny's strong will was accustomed to bear down all impediments in its way. With one arm thrown round Morris's neck (for she knew how such caresses were valued by her old nurse), she poured out in her own energetic, glowing language, the story of the young dress-maker's sorrows and wrongs—until she succeeded in her object of enlisting the warm, womanly sympathies of her listener in Grace Arnold's favour.

"I am sure you will do all I want you, kind Morris. You know that I am a spoiled child, and must always be allowed to have my own way. First, then, I shall want you to pack me a basket of good things—wine, arrowroot, jellies, grapes, everything that is likely to be needed by the sick. You will know best." And as she spoke, she poured out the contents of her purse on Morris's knee, stopping all her prudent remonstrances with a kiss; "Be sure you make haste, Morris; there's an old dear; for there is no time to lose. While you are gone, I will be getting ready, and send Pedro for a coach."

"Dear, dear, Miss Fanny! this is just like you!" exclaimed the old nurse, with a warning shake of the head, as the young lady paused to take breath. "It's no use anybody trying to give you advice; you won't be crossed. It was just so when you was a child. You would have kept all the beggar children in the village on pension if you could; and your poor dear mamma was the same. You had always a way of your own that people could never get over. If you have made up your mind to see this young woman to-night, I know that you will go, in spite of everything."

"And you will go with me, Morris," returned

Fanny, with a confident air; "you cannot hide your kind heart from me, if you try ever so much."

The heart of the old nurse fluttered with pleasure at this proof of the estimation in which she was held by her darling. She gathered up the money which was still scattered on her knee, counted it carefully, then began bustling about for her bonnet and cloak, as eager and almost as impatient as Fanny herself. But her benevolent pleasure in the performance of a kind act was, it is true, a little alloyed by the human triumph of making Mrs. Foster ashamed of herself, and proving to her that everyone was not so selfish and cold hearted; for between that lady and Morris there had always existed a secret feud. The faithful, but somewhat eccentric old servant, deserved the confidence of her mistress, and proved her fitness to be the agent of the young lady's generosity. The needful purchases were made, and the basket quietly packed, in less time than it would have taken some people to decide how it was to be done.

Pedro procured a coach for Miss Templeton, accomplishing his errand with more than usual promptness—possibly stimulated by a liberal donation to himself—which was rendered doubly acceptable by the fact that Mrs. Foster kept a very tight rein over her establishment.

Fanny found the little servant just as she left her, seated most uncomfortably on the extreme edge of one of the chairs nearest the door, examining the room in furtive, awe-struck glances, and growing every moment more miserable; for the possession of the half-crown could not make her insensible to the fear that Miss Grace would think her loitering on the way; and the anger of her mistress loomed most unpleasantly in the back ground.

Fanny compassionately reassured the poor girl, and kindly telling her to follow, she piloted the unfortunate black bonnet through the hall with imperturbable dignity; suspecting as she did, the concealed proximity of the prying, giggling servants, and conscious that this whim of hers would be a staple fund of amusement for them. But the heiress minded this quite as little as she did the sentimental fondling of her Aunt, or the awkward love-making of her luckless swain, George Foster, who, much as he wished to obey his mother's private instructions, generally betrayed a disposition to run away from the young lady; the impression always presenting itself to his obtuse brain, that the little vixen was making fun of him.

There was a power of independent antagonism in Fanny Templeton's character, that made her delight in rebelling against established authorities, and breaking through conventional rules and customs.

## CHAPTER V.

The evening wore away very wearily to Grace Arnold, watching by her father's bedside, and awaiting the return of her messenger, in feverish anxiety to know the result of her appeal to Mrs. Foster. The invalid still slept, but she found it impossible to rest, or settle down to any occupation. She could only watch, and wait, with her nerves painfully vibrating to every sound. Susan seemed to have been gone a very long time; perhaps she had missed her way; or, worse, she might have lost the letter.

Grace rose and went to the window, pressing her hand upon her burning brow, as if no longer able to endure the torturing thoughts. The suspense, with its heart-sickening alternations of hope and despair, was becoming almost intolerable.

"Hark! what was that?" Grace hurriedly dropped the corner of the window blind, and started eagerly forward. A step on the stairs. She knew that it was not Susan's, and could have wept at the disappointment.

A man's foot! Perhaps it was one of the other lodgers. No! It came up gropingly, as if the person was not certain of his locality, nor familiar with the dark stairs. Then she heard the sharp shrill voice of the officious landlady directing the stranger to their room.

Grace cast one loving, apprehensive look at the bed, but to her great relief, the noise had not disturbed her father. There she stood, only a few paces from the door, watching it with heaving bosom, and widely dilated eyes, her sweet, firm mouth painfully compressed, and twitching at the corners; a strange, despairing look, that seemed to cast the shadows of twenty additional years on her young face.

The prolonged absence of Susan, her letter to Mrs. Foster, all were forgotten now. The vague dread in which she had lived for the last few weeks, was now resolving itself into a still more terrible reality. She felt that a great crisis of her life was near.

There was a quick, assured rap at the door. Grace could not have said, come in, to the intruder, if her life had depended on her uttering those two words. But the visitor did not wait for an invitation, he opened the door, and entered unbidden.

A little, lean, wiry, old man, with a dry, pinched face, like a frost bitten crab; keen, distrustful, grey eyes, which when he was angered, seemed to have a green light in them; a hard, selfish mouth, and a smile, that was even more ill-favoured than his frown. Grace knew him; her foreboding instinct had not deceived her. It was Harry Clare's uncle—the man who had stepped so ruthlessly between her and happiness, and who held such power to torture her, through her love to her dying father. He was just the man to make the most of his advantage. He would use his power. The first glance at his face, impressed this conviction on Grace. She felt that it would be useless, either to appeal to his pity, or hope for any awakening of human feeling, in a heart so world hardened, and narrowed to the pursuit of its own selfish aims.

The Arnolds were unfortunate and poor; that was enough to exclude them from his sympathy; for poverty and misfortune were the two capital offences which he never forgave. When a man had sinned in this way, he was never regarded by him with anything but hatred and suspicion. Like a great many of his well-to-do brethren in the world, he reserved the right hand of fellowship, for the successful, and the prosperous; parted with his money, only when he was sure of its being refunded at compound interest, and subscribed largely to the theory, that when a man is down, he must be kept down.

Grace felt a sick faintness coming over her; but the physical weakness was resolutely struggled against. It was the thought of her father, that nerved her strong heart. For his sake, she would need all her courage. "If I give way now, what will become of him?" It was this, that sustained her; for, at whatever cost of pain, or personal sacrifice, she alone must stand between him, and this pitiless persecutor.

There was a glass of cold water standing on the little table, just within reach of her hand; she seized it, and drank with feverish eagerness. The cool timely draught revived her; she could bear the worst now, firm in the simple, religious faith, that formed one of the strong points of her character. Faith to believe, that the all merciful Disposer of events would impose no burden that it was beyond her strength to bear.

Old Matthew Clare watched her curiously. He remembered Grace Arnold well. When he first met her, it was in her father's elegant villa; and she was doing the hospitable honours to the guests, at his well appointed table. The contrast between that time and the present struck him forcibly; but it only served to confirm him in his relentless determination, that his nephew should not throw away his prospects in life, for the sake of a beggarly bankrupt's daughter. What Grace might suffer in the separation, he never took into account; what had she to do with feelings? they were not for people in her position!

He had already contrived to interrupt the correspondence of the lovers. It was during the young man's absence, that Mr. Arnold and his daughter had been compelled to remove to their present poor lodging. Harry's ignorance of their address, had obliged him to enclose his letters to Grace, under cover, to his uncle; not for a moment suspecting that his trust would be betrayed.

Grace never received the letters, which would have saved her many a heart-ache. But Harry was on his way home. It was now Matthew Clare's purpose to prevent (if possible) a meeting between his nephew and Grace; for he knew that an explanation would unmask his own treachery and defeat all his cherished plans. He knew enough of Grace Arnold to convince him that with her a promise would be sacred; he had only to work upon her love, and fears for her father, to wring from her this pledge; when it was once given, he knew that he could trust her to the end. It was for this, he had sought them in their obscure retreat, which could scarcely be called a home. What was there about that tall, slight girl, that made him feel so disconcerted in her presence? He was angry with himself, for allowing her to impress him in such a way.

She stood confronting him with her graceful head erect, her figure drawn up to its full height, and her clear, brown eyes looking at him in that odd scrutinizing way that in spite of himself, made him feel abashed and uncomfortable. He could not understand her. Was it defiance? Had they money to meet his demand? If it had been a question concerning the foreclosing of a coveted mortgage, he could not have felt more nervously anxious.

Still Grace stood waiting for him to speak, pale, proud, and self-collected; but with wild waves of agony surging over her heart. She would have endured more than this, rather than betray, to that relentless old man, what it cost her to preserve her outward calmness.

He crossed his wrinkled hands on the knob of his thick, yellow walking stick, cleared his throat by a short, dry, preliminary cough, and peering vindictively at Grace, from beneath his bent brows, he assumed a confidence that he was far from feeling, and began, in a high pitched, quavering voice:—

"Miss Arnold, madam—I can see that the sight of me is not at all welcome to you. Whether my visit is to end more agreeably than it has commenced, depends entirely on yourself. Of course you have read my letter. Miss Arnold, you know me, and your father knows me, to be a plain man of few words; but always prompt and to the point. Well now, what I want to know is whether you are willing to avail yourself of my offer in your father's favour?"

His words were like sharp pointed arrows, not one missed aim.

Grace breathed hard, and her face whitened, but she did not droop or lower her eyes. She looked only a little colder and prouder, as she pointed, meaningly, towards the bed, answering him in a low, suppressed voice, that sounded husky and unnatural even to herself:—

"Be careful, Mr. Clare; my father is very

ill. If possible, I would spare him the pain of this scene. If he wakes now, and sees you here, I cannot say what might be the consequence of this most ill-timed visit."

"In that case I should be sorry, Miss Arnold, for I mean no harm either to you or your father."

And, dropping his voice almost to a whisper, he immediately changed his tactics; adopting a persuasive, conciliating manner, that was even more repulsive to the sensitive, high-minded Grace.

"Come, you are a sensible girl, and as far as I have been able to judge, you have always proved yourself a good daughter, I think you will act as such now. Mark, it is not my wish that your father should be disturbed. All I want is simply your written promise that my nephew and yourself shall in future be strangers to each other. Just a few words, a line will be enough, signed by your hand. It will be merely a form, to satisfy Harry's conscience, and, in return, I will cancel my claim upon your father, and hand over to you the promissory note, in virtue of which I can now, or at any time, send him to a debtor's prison."

He seemed to gloat over the words with malicious pleasure, the exulting gleam in his eyes being a strange contradiction to his coaxing manner.

"And if I refuse?" said Grace, in the same low, constrained voice in which she had before spoken; "if my heart and reason both force me to deny your right to extort such a bond, what then?"

"What then?" he repeated, clutching his stick tightly, and catching his breath in a sort of spasm; his face kindling into a dull, white heat, in his fury of suppressed passion, "Why you will compel me to proceed to extremities; unless your father can discharge his debt by twelve o'clock to-morrow, a writ shall be served against him.

At last Grace showed she was moved. She started, glanced shudderingly at the bed, and answered, with a painful trembling in her voice:—

"You could not be so cruel, sir, in my father's present condition! Oh! you will not, if you are a man and a Christian! I cannot believe it, even of you."

"What have I to do with your father's condition? If his own daughter will not save him from a prison, when she may do it by a few strokes of her pen, what can he claim from me?"

The scene was becoming almost too much for the already severely tried powers of Grace. Her heart was beating wildly, and her brain was in a whirl; she caught the back of a chair, and leaned heavily against it for support.

"Your money shall be paid to the utmost farthing, only grant us time," she pleaded, lifting her eyes earnestly to his face. It was the last time that she ever ventured an appeal to that stony heart.

He smiled, his own sinister, ill-favoured

smile. All the evil in his nature was roused now.

"No, not a day, nor an hour beyond the time I have fixed. I will have no half-measures, consent to no terms but those I have offered. You must choose between them. Refuse, and a prison for your father is the only alternative. Mark me, Grace Arnold, I would not lightly barter good hard cash for a girl's promise. But I would do anything to save my adopted son from being drawn into a marriage against his better judgment, because his honour will not suffer him to be the first to break up an intimacy which ought never to have been regarded but as a piece of boyish folly."

It was a daring random shot, but it told as he had anticipated.

Grace started, and recoiled as if she had received a blow, and a film seemed to creep over her eyes. But she bit her lip to hide its quivering, and cleared her voice by a powerful effort of self-command.

"Drawn into a marriage against his better judgment, did you say, sir? Am I to understand that you spoke on your nephew's authority, and that he has empowered you to act for him in this? Tell me the truth, as you ever hope to have it told to you. Has Harry Clare chosen this method of dissolving an engagement which he has found himself unable to fulfil?"

For a moment the plotting old uncle hesitated, and trembled for the after consequences of his cruel falsehood, when he thought of his impetuous, high-spirited nephew, and remembered his letters to Grace, which breathed all the unabated fervour and fire of a passion which neither time, absence, nor change of scene, had been able to influence. But he had now gone too far to retract. It was still his inflexible resolution to separate Harry from this girl, whom he now hated, (not only for the trouble she was causing him,) but for the brave high spirit which she had retained in the midst of her poverty.

"Well, since you force it from me, I will be open with you; but, remember, I would have spared you this. Yes, it is my nephew's wish that this engagement should be broken off. He is older, has seen a little more of the world, and I fancy there is some other attachment. We often see such changes. But you know Harry, Miss Arnold. He fancies himself bound to you, and will sacrifice himself to a scruple of honour."

"It is unnecessary," said Grace, in a changed voice, that sounded unnaturally clear and cold, making a desperate effort to keep down a choking feeling in her throat; "your nephew is free, Mr. Clare. I am sorry that he has felt himself obliged to have recourse to such means of communicating his wishes. He has done me cruel injustice if he supposed that I should ever make use of our engagement to exact from him a sacrifice, either of interest or inclination."

The crafty grey eyes lit up with sudden exultation. That last cunning stroke had been successful even beyond his calculation. He knew now how to deal with the strange girl, and felt himself on surer ground; still the victory was but half-won. Mr. Arnold's illness alarmed him; if he died before he could secure his hold upon Grace, he foresaw that all his schemes would be frustrated It was not without some secret misgiving that he ventured to say:

"You are right, Grace Arnold, and I thank you for my nephew's sake. Only give me your written assurance that he is free, (as far as you are concerned) and I withdraw all claim upon your father; not that I doubt your word, but it will be better to have some proof—more like business. And as your knowledge of my nephew's altered feelings will now remove any objection that might have withheld—"

Grace had moved to the table, and with her beautiful face hardening into a look of white, stony rigidness, was searching mechanically for pen, ink, and paper.

The old man was speaking with trembling eagerness, when his words were abruptly cut short by a sudden cry from the bed:

"Grace, Grace, where are you?"

The sound of her father's voice, instantly recalled the poor girl's wandering senses, and warmed back to life the frozen currents of feeling and thought.

"I am here, dear father: I have never left you," and she sprang to his bedside, intent only upon one purpose—to soothe her father, and if possible, keep him in merciful ignorance of all that had happened. But it was too late; he had already seen and recognised their visitor, and the consciousness of his errand was recalled to him in an overpowering flood of painful thoughts. His mind seemed to gather in at once an instinctive knowledge of all that Grace wished to conceal. He raised himself in bed by an almost supernatural effort. His eyes kindled, and the tones of his voice, filled out with commanding power, as he laid a firm hand on his daughter's arm.

She looked at him wonderingly. For the moment all his strength seemed restored to him. It was the last expiring flash of the torch before it sinks for ever.

"You have not disobeyed me, girl? Tell me, you have not bound yourself by any rash promise?"

"No, dear father, no," Grace murmured faintly, her slight figure trembling like a reed in the excess of her agitation, for the strength which had sustained her through the trying scene was now giving way. Harry Clare had ever been such a favourite of her father's. He esteemed and trusted him so highly. How could she awaken him from his delusion, and confess that Harry was not what they had believed him; that he had deceived them both, and that the love which had been the sunlight of her own lonely life was now only a dream of the past.

"John Arnold!" It was Mr. Clare's voice raised threateningly. He had recovered from the passion of disappointed rage into which he had been thrown by this little scene between father and daughter; and suspecting that Grace had purposely deceived him about her father's illness, he advanced to the foot of the bed, his stick planted resolutely on the floor, glaring at them with a cruel menace in his eyes. But before he could proceed, Grace was at his side, her hand laid firmly on his arm, and her voice raised commandingly,

"Not another word, sir; this scene will kill my father. You must not—shall not stay here. You have no legal authority for this cruel persecution of a dying man. I will not appeal to your pity, for I know now that it would be worse than useless. I will urge the only argument that is likely to reach natures such as yours. For your own sake, then, leave us, if you would not have the stain of murder on your grey hairs, and if you would save the remnant of your days from the bitterest self-reproach."

"Come away, Grace," cried the sick man, with sudden passion. "Let him carry out his threats. I do not fear him. A prison has no terrors for—"

But even while he spoke a change passed over his face. His voice faltered and fell. There was a painful gasping for breath, then a choking gurgling in his throat, and he sank back on his pillow, where he lay ghastly pale and almost pulseless. A dark stream of blood gushing from his white lips, and making a crimson stain upon the coverlet.

Grace sprang to her father with a sharp, agonizing cry that seemed to rend her heart strings, hung over him for an instant, laid her cheek to his, as if the fond action had some power of healing in it, and her strong love could turn the ebbing tide of vitality, and reanimate the sinking frame with some of her own young life.

It was at this moment that the sound of whispering voices and hurried footsteps on the stairs caught the ear of old Matthew Clare, which was now tremblingly alive to every sound. He had shrank away from the bed in his fright, and was in the act of opening the door, intent only upon his present object—a hasty retreat from the wretched place. He was now haunted by a vague fear that something unpleasant to himself might result from his visit. Grace Arnold might accuse him before the people in the house, who might take the law of punishment into their own hands. He knew there were usually some desperate characters in these poor lodging-houses.

This was the scene which awaited the benevolent heiress and her old nurse, who, guided by Susan, quickened their steps through the scream from Grace, and found themselves in the home of the poor young dressmaker.

## CHAPTER VI.

More than an hour had passed since old Matthew Clare had turned from the sick room, and crept down the dark stairs, feeling his dignity very much diminished in its proportions, and oppressed by a most uncomfortable and unusual feeling of self-dissatisfaction. He mentally cursed the adverse fate which had contrived such a meeting between himself and Miss Fanny Templeton. That young lady was not unknown to him; he had met her several times in company with her eccentric old uncle Lomax, the rich Indian nabob, who had made her his heiress. It was natural that the old man should have thought of her as one of the matrimonial prizes he was anxious to secure for his nephew, for he had, of course, never calculated the possibility of Grace Arnold and the whimsical little heiress becoming known to each other. He foresaw that this unlucky acquaintance would effectually destroy any hopes that he might have formed in that direction.

His difficulties were also increased, for the next eligible name on his list was a prim, faded maiden, of uncertain age, the daughter of a deceased partner. In point of fortune, she was nearly equal to Miss Templeton, but he had a secret misgiving that the lady herself would not exactly suit his nephew's fastidious taste.

The night was clear and frosty. The outlines of the tall houses on the opposite side of the narrow street were defined sharp and clear in the cold pale light of the unclouded winter moon. The wind was rising with a sobbing, wailing sound, like the moaning of grieved spirits.

Those who had homes to go to were instinctively hurrying to seek their kindly shelter, and the busy, waking sounds of life were dying away.

A stillness like the shadow of death had fallen on the little group of watchers by the bedside of Mr. Arnold.

No time had been lost in summoning the attendance of the nearest medical man. And Fanny recollecting that Dr. Marsh was at that time in London,—he was an old family friend and neighbour, and had been dear uncle Lomax's favourite physician for many years,—she wrote and despatched a hasty note, which by rare good fortune found him at home. The kind old doctor came at once, and did all that could be done for the patient, who was already beyond the power of the healing art. The practised hands of Morris had effected a decided improvement in the outward aspect of things. The basket had been quietly unpacked, and its various delicacies unostentatiously disposed the table.

There was wine now—everything that the sick man had so vainly craved—but it had come too late to be of any avail. Morris seemed to understand exactly what was required by her new position. She assumed the direction of everything, and dropped at once into her self-imposed duties as nurse, taking upon herself with gentle womanly tact the burden which she saw that the heart-stricken daughter was no longer able to bear.

The good creature had some natural scruples about the propriety of her young lady's prolonged absence from her aunt's, which at present was to be regarded as her home; but Fanny had answered them by sitting down at once to write to Mrs. Foster, as usual taking the decision of the matter into her own hands.

"I must stay here, good Morris; I feel that it is my duty. My life has been like a pleasant dream. I have been kept too much in ignorance of the misery and suffering there is in the world. No, I cannot leave this poor girl."

All this was poured out in an undertone to Morris, whose only reply was a fond pressure of the hand, a dubious shake of the head, and a silently-invoked blessing on the head of her wilful young mistress.

Grace sat by her father's bed, her hand closely locked in his clasp, from which she dared not withdraw it for fear of disturbing his position. Her eyes wandered round the room with a passive, unquestioning kind of wonder, unable to realize anything beyond the consciousness that her father was well cared for by these benevolent strangers; but mutely looking the thanks she could not speak, with her heart too full even for the relief of tears. So the silent hours crept on.

The white shrunken face upon the pillow looked so still and motionless, and the feeble fluttering breath seemed to become fainter every moment. More than once a chill of foreboding fear crept to the heart of Grace, as she felt the cold, damp fingers tightening almost convulsively over her own.

At last there was a feeble stirring of the bed clothes. The dim eyes were slowly unclosed and fastened wistfully on Grace, and a gleam of returning consciousness flashed like a passing light over the face. The sick man made a painful effort to speak, but it was with difficulty that the anxiously-strained ear of the listener caught his whispered words.

"Come nearer, Grace. It is getting so dark and cold, darling. I have seen—your—mother. And—little Charley. They are—waiting for me—in—the better land. And I am going! Do not grieve, my kind one, your—mother will know—all you—have—been to me. Nearer—nearer yet, Grace. I cannot—see—you now. My last treasure! God bless and—"

His voice sank into an indistinct murmur. He had something more to say. Grace guessed what it was, for she fancied once that she caught the name of Harry Clare. But it was too late; his feeble thread of life was broken. Grace felt the clasp upon her hand relax, and saw the heavy eyelids droop and fall. So, with his heart still clinging to her, and the broken prayer for her upon his lips, his spirit drifted out to the shore of the unknown world.

"Oh, father, take me with you!" moaned the poor orphan, burying her face in the coverlet; "I have no place now in this dreary world. There is no one to miss me or need my love," and under the aching sense of sudden desolation the much tried heart gave way as it had never done under all the blighting cares of poverty, and in the bitter world struggles which the devoted daughter had so bravely met for the sake of the parent who had been so helplessly dependent on her love.

But now that there was no longer this necessity for self-sacrifice, no longer the sustaining purpose which had carried her through so many trying scenes with a power of endurance which had sometimes surprised even herself, with the shock of her father's death came the natural re-action which at once prostrated the over-worn powers of body and mind. The poor girl fainted by the side of her dead father. From that moment she remembered nothing. For many weary weeks life was a blank, filled only with restless dreams. Kind hands removed her to her own little bed in the inner room, for the long death-like swoon alarmed even the experienced Morris. The physician was hastily recalled. He shook his head gravely in answer to Fanny's anxious questioning, and, turning aside to Morris, urged the pressing necessity for the poor girl's removal to a larger and more airy room.

Immediate application was made to the landlady, who willingly consented to prepare at once a room on her second floor, which by good fortune chanced to be vacant. She was stimulated into this sudden graciousness by the prospect of liberal payment, and the discovery that the poor dressmaker had friends of such consequence.

Fanny bent over the unconscious girl in an agony of distress. Her friendless, unprotected condition, the manner in which she was thus thrown upon the mercy of strangers, and more than all, the touching story which she had herself heard of her gentle goodness and devotion to her father.

Everything combined to plead strongly for Grace in the mind of the generous, impulsive Fanny. It was just the sort of appeal to which her quick, womanly sympathies would be certain to respond. Then she remembered that Grace was, like herself, an orphan. This seemed to establish a kindred bond between them. It was in that solemn hour, before the calm smile had faded from the silent lips of the dead—while Grace still lay in that swoon, so near akin to death, and it remained a question of sorrowful doubt whether the weary young head would ever be raised again—that Fanny Templeton registered in her own heart a silent vow that, if it pleased God to spare Grace Arnold, she would be to her always a friend and sister, and that the dreary, hopeless days of ill-paid, life-wasting toil should be known to her no more.

Before morning the poor girl's illness had assumed a decided form. Morris had her worst fears confirmed by the old doctor, who informed her, with characteristic candour, that it was a most violent attack of brain fever, that the young person was in great danger, and that he considered it advisable for Miss Fanny to leave the house as soon as possible. This last suggestion the young lady was at first disposed to indignantly reject, protesting, with sparkling tears in her black eyes, that she was not the least afraid of infection, and would do nothing so cruel and cowardly as to desert the poor girl in her present extremity for the sake of a mere selfish fear. But the tearful, imploring entreaties of her faithful old servant, and the wise counsel and kindly firmness of her friend, the doctor, at last prevailed; and satisfied that she would be allowed to provide for the invalid's wants as liberally as she pleased, and consoled by the thought that she would be well cared for in the hands of Morris, Fanny reluctantly consented to go back in the carriage which had been sent for her, with the page Pedro bearing a scented note from his mistress, in which that lady chose to consider herself personally slighted by her niece's extraordinary conduct in leaving her house in the manner she had done on the previous evening. Miss Foster had also added a few delicate lines, as a postcript to her mother's letter, in which she expressed much dignified surprise and regret that cousin Fanny should have so far forgotten her position, as to allow a rash impulse of misguided generosity to lead her into a proceeding so improper and unladylike.

At any other time this would have provoked a stinging, defiant retort from Fanny, and her high spirit would have risen in instant rebellion. But now, as she finished reading the obnoxious note, she only wrinkled her broad brow a little and gave her pretty mouth the slightest possible curve of scorn, then quietly refolded it, and continued her parting talk to the old servant as if the note and its writer had entirely passed from her mind.

"It is best to go back at once, Miss Fanny," Morris whispered, as she carefully adjusted her young lady's cloak and veil, "or Mrs. Foster will be writing off to your Aunt Margaret, and frightening the poor lady out of her senses about you."

"Dear Aunt Margaret," murmured Fanny, regretfully, "she will miss me so much. I would go back to her to-morrow, if it was not for this poor Grace Arnold. I am beginning to love her already. Dear Morris, I commit her to your kind care; you will try your best to save her."

With her manner unusually subdued, the shadow of the death-scene still lingering solemnly in her thoughts, and a host of good and softening influences already beginning to act upon her vividly impressionable nature, the heiress went back to her Aunt Foster's, while Morris, by her own benevolent wish, remained behind to nurse poor Grace. Old Dr. Marsh, Fanny's staunch friend and supporter whenever it pleased her to be indebted to him, kindly relieved her of a pressing weight of responsibility by voluntarily taking into his own hands the arrangements for Mr. Arnold's funeral. He directed all the solemn preparations, and gained Miss Templeton's lasting esteem and gratitude by the delicate manner in which he paid the final tribute of respect to the memory of an unfortunate gentleman who had sinned against the world in nothing but his failures and his poverty.

While the sable-plumed hearse, with its stately black horses, was slowly bearing the remains of her father to their last resting-place, Grace was restlessly tossing on her fevered pillow, unconscious of the bereavement which had broken her last kindred tie, and of the kind Providence who had sent such friends in the hour of need, and was ever surrounding her with such tender care.

The same frosty, wintry sunshine that lingered on her father's grave and gleamed on his coffin as they were lowering it into darkness, struggled into the room where the sick girl lay, wandered over her pillow in pale, feeble rays, quivered upon her burning hands, and seemed to bring a brighter crimson to her flushed cheek. Grace was living again in the past. The death-shadowed present had melted away like a night mist before the rising dawn. Dreams had restored all that she had lost. The vanished light of other days, the unbroken home circle, the dear household loves; all were given back; and, lastly, that one deep love of later time to which her woman's heart had unfolded itself as a budding flower opens to the first kiss of sunlight, the love which had made her world so fair, and in which she had lived such a full, and perfect life. It was touching to listen to her ravings, softened as they were into the gentle prattle that partook of all her native sweetness. She talked of her mother in low, loving words, that lingered long on the theme, and showed how yearningly the poor weary heart turned back to the old days; it was touching to see how faithfully memory reproduced the scenes on which it dwelt, how she fancied herself again kneeling with shyly averted face before her mother's low rocking-chair, pouring her first maiden confessions into the patient ear of that beloved listener, and receiving the whispered blessing on herself and Harry Clare with a rapture that found expression in a burst of tears and kisses. But this happy mood changed suddenly; the patient grew more restless and excited; the name of Harry Clare was oftener on her lips, and it always seemed to call up a doubting, troubled look. Darker threads were woven with the tangled web of thought. Her recollections became more confused and fragmentary. The connecting chain of events was lost in a strange blending of the present and the past. She would often press her hand wearily to her forehead, as if to remove some painful weight, and her beautiful, wandering eyes would follow the quietly-moving figure of Morris, and sometimes she would hold out her hand with trembling eagerness, saying,

"I do not know you, but it seems as if you had been here a long time. I like you because your voice is low and kind like my mother's. Perhaps she has sent you here."

"Dear heart! dear heart!" murmured Morris, compassionately, holding a cooling draught to the parched lips.

Grace made a sudden movement that nearly over-turned the glass, and its contents:

"Hush! what were you saying about Harry Clare? I will not believe a word against him; you would not talk so if you knew him better. I know he has not written once since he went away, and they say he has forgotten me. But I love him, yes; I love him still, and I will trust him to the end. I cannot promise to give him up, my father has forbidden me; but his uncle must be paid by some means. Yes, I will go to Mrs. Foster, and tell her all. You must not hinder me from getting up now, for I have Mrs. Foster's dress to finish before I can take it. I was so frightened just now, for I thought that I had lost her patterns."

Nerved by the wild energy of fever, Grace attempted to rise, and it required all the soothing powers of the nurse to combat this resolution.

It was these unconscious revelations of the invalid, that gradually helped Morris to a clearer insight into the family history of the Arnold's, and it was in this way that she became possessed of the precious secret which poor Grace had ever guarded so jealously. But the knowledge thus gained by Morris was most religiously preserved from every one else, with, of course, the single exception of her young mistress, from whom she could conceal nothing. But she was scrupulously careful never to allow any prying strangers in the sick room, a measure which received the doctor's decided approbation. He had a very high opinion of Morris, though she herself knew it not. He respected her, not merely for the qualities that made her invaluable as a nurse, but because she had (in his eyes) the rare feminine merit of talking very little, and that little always to the point. It was for this that he paid her the compliment of setting her down among the few sensible women whom he had met in the course of his life.

Dear Old Morris, would she have fallen in the estimation of the pretendedly cynical, but really kind-hearted, doctor, if he had watched her as she sat listening to poor Grace's feverish ramblings, and observed how often she raised the corner of her apron and stealthily wiped her eyes. She took a strange tender interest in the touching story which she had gleaned at intervals from the frequent allusions to Harry Clare. There was something in that half-revealed story of love to which her own heart could vibrate in sympathy, for Morris (unmistakeable old maid as she was) had once been young and pretty; even her simple uneventful life had had its seasoning of sweet romance. There was a little hoard of treasured relics hidden away with jealous care; the half of a broken sixpence, an old-fashioned locket shrining a curl of dark hair, and a parcel of yellow old letters tied together with a faded blue ribbon, which testified her life's constancy to the gallant sailor lover whose grave lay in a far-off distant land. Yes, Morris had had her love dream, as most women have; for few, let us hope, have to look wearily back on the barren, desolate experience of a life which has ripened and faded from the opening spring bud to the seared autumn leaf with the heart still a stranger to the sweet human joy of loving and being loved.

Every day found the nurse more attached to her charge; and, if possible, more devoted and untiring in her care. As the dreaded crisis of the disorder approached there was something almost painful in the anxiety with which she watched for any sign of hope in the doctor's face.

Very near to the shadowy confines of the spirit world passed Grace. But the fiat had not yet gone forth, her life of love and duty was not to end here; there was other work for her to do. She was not to die.

There was quite a little jubilee in the sick room, on the first day that Grace was able to leave her bed, and be dressed to receive Miss Templeton, for Dr. Marsh had at last withdrawn his prohibition, and the impatient Fanny was allowed to visit her. Poor little Susan had been twice caught by her mistress on the stairs, giving expression to her feelings in a variety of extravagant demonstrations that would have drawn down upon her a summary rebuke but for the rare chance that her mistress was on that day disposed to feel unusually amiable. Poor child, she had a right to rejoice in the sick girl's recovery.

None knew except Morris how often she had robbed herself of needful sleep during Grace's illness, for the nurse had several times been startled to find her crouching in a dark corner of the landing, crying quietly to herself.

Fanny Templeton could scarcely restrain her tears when she found herself holding one of the invalid's wasted hands, and listening to the weak voice addressing her timidly by name, and trying to thank her. It was to Fanny the most difficult task of all to succeed in diverting the poor girl's gratitude from herself; for Grace seemed to have gathered, by a sort of intuition a knowledge of all that she owed to the timely benevolence of Mrs. Foster's niece. She could not trust herself to speak much of her father, for they had been united by such close bonds of affection, and the anguish of his loss was still too keenly felt; nor could she suffer her mind to dwell upon the last painful scene with Mr. Clare, which the first dawning consciousness of reality had recalled to her. She was still too feeble, both in body and mind, for any return of mental excitement not to be attended with danger.

Before Fanny took leave of Grace that day she had formed in her own mind a certain plan, which was matured in a private consultation with old Dr. Marsh, at the end of which he shook her warmly by the hand, and protested that henceforth little "Fire Flash," this was his favorite name for Fanny, might be as wild and whimsical as she pleased, he should never find fault with her. Then he rubbed his bald head with a comically puzzled air, and after a thoughtful pinch of snuff, returned to his original theory, that women, old or young, were all riddles.

Fanny Templeton sat up late that night to write to her Aunt Margaret. Not until she had begun and finished a long, earnest letter, could she think of composing herself to sleep; for setting it down upon paper seemed to her to advance her a step nearer to the fulfilment of the scheme on which she had set her heart.

It was to take Grace Arnold home with her to Woodlands. This was the name of the house which she had inherited from her Uncle Lomax, and which was presided over by his maiden sister, Fanny's only surviving relative on the maternal side.

"Dear Aunt Maggie," she wrote, "you, who never refused me anything, I know I may count upon you for consent to one of the few wise propositions which I ever made. I would not take such a step without consulting you, for, dear as this scheme has already become to me, I would give it up at once, if I thought you would not approve of it. But I feel sure you will, darling aunty; there are so many excellent reasons why you should. I have already told you all I know of poor Grace's history, enough, I know, to ensure her a kind welcome at Woodlands. She must come; she will never recover her strength while she stays in those stifling city lodgings. And, for the rest, you will soon love her for herself, and she will deserve to be so loved.

Your old friend, Dr. Marsh, is prepared to confirm all I say in her favour. And then, aunty, must I confess it? I have some selfish views of my own. I feel so much the want of a companion of my own age. You, yourself, have often regretted that the society around Woodlands was not more to my taste. For I have all dear Uncle Lomax's aversion to the conventional, model young ladies who are manufactured to order in the genteel boarding schools, and come out, in the fulness of time, without an idea beyond Berlin wool patterns, indifferent music, and bad French. There will be something elevating in association with a good, earnest creature like Grace Arnold. Hers is a character worth studying; for, humble as her present position is, I am convinced that she is a perfect English lady in all the most important essentials for the title, education, moral training, and habits of thought."

This was the purport of Fanny's long letter, to which was added a modest postscript, next morning.

"Forgive me, dear Aunt Maggie, but I must exact from you a little more indulgence. You will remember that I told you I had gained my information about Grace through a little servant girl called Susan. Grace Arnold has been kind to her. I fear kindness has been rare to the poor little thing. She has evinced so much grateful affection in return that I feel quite interested in her future fate, for I hear from Morris that she has a very hard place. If I could only persuade you aunt, to receive the poor thing into your happy domestic kingdom, and let her be placed under old Nancy, our cook, I am sure little Susan will turn out well. I had quite an argument about it the other day with my cousin Alice, who contends that the lower classes are hopelessly vicious and depraved. Good bye, dear Aunt Maggie. I am heartily tired of this visit, and longing to get back to Woodlands. How are all my pets, 'Keeper,' and 'Dash,' and 'Jip,' the parrot, and my mare 'Juno?' I hope Driver takes care of her."

No time was lost in despatching this all important letter; and Fanny, full of her secret, prudently decided that in the present early stage of proceedings it would be impolitic to take any of the Foster family into her confidence.

## CHAPTER VII.

It was on a dull wet morning, about three weeks after the date of Fanny Templeton's letter to her Aunt Margaret, that Alice Foster, with scornful indignation in her looks and an open letter in her hand, sailed majestically into the room where her mother and her brother George were holding a little private conversation, which, to judge by Mrs. Foster's clouded brow and general irritability of manner, was anything but agreeable or satisfactory to that lady. The truth was that she had been entertaining her son with a small piece of her mind relative to a certain family disappointment in which he was concerned: this was nothing less than the ignominious failure of one of her numerous attempts at match making; the frustration of her darling scheme of getting her niece's fortune into the family. For Fanny Templeton had positively rejected her son's suit on the evening before the day of her return home, when luckless George Foster, goaded by his sister's sneers at his want of courage, and secretly stimulated by the artful persuasions of his mother, who had at last succeeded in impressing him with the idea that the young lady was really in love with him, and that he had only to speak and conquer, had wound up his small mind to the proposing point, and on the evening in question actually made his cousin Fanny an offer of marriage in the back drawing-room, where his mother had cleverly contrived that they should be left alone together.

If Mrs. Foster had rightly estimated the character of her niece she would never have committed the mistake of seeking to make such a match for any of her sons. Fanny disliked them all. If she had any slight preference it was in favour of George, who had the merit of being less vain and more good-natured than either of his brothers. But that her aunt should interpret this as the expression of some warmer feeling, that it should ever have been supposed that she could accept him as her husband was more than she could bear.

Fanny did not know whether to laugh or cry at the absurdity of the jest which had been practised upon her. George Foster was certainly the most unlikely subject that could have been chosen for the ideal fancy of a girl like Fanny Templeton. There was something too gross and material about him; the presence of the animal was too broadly recognisable.

He had a heavy, clownish figure, and a full, florid face, without any whiskers to give it a relieving shadow, and sleek, straight, light hair, that gave him an indescribable dash of sheepishness. Such was Mrs. Foster's second son, whom his brothers voted confoundedly slow and his father sometimes called a fool, and who was scouted as stupid by his sister's young lady friends. But his mother, to do her justice, always took the slighted young gentleman under the shelter of her maternal wing, and showed her preference by reserving for him the brilliant destiny of marrying the heiress of Woodlands.

That he had not been gratefully sensible of this distinction, and had neglected to improve his advantages, was now made a subject of irritating reproach to him. It was true that he had from the first shown a most unlover-like reluctance to press his suit with the lady, of whose unmerciful wit he had always stood in awe. He could be occasionally brilliant on the merits of horses and dogs, was initiated in all the mysteries of the turf, and conversant with the exploits of gentlemen of the prize ring, besides being well read up in the sporting literature of the day, but he had a dim perception that all this did not qualify him for the society of his cousin Fanny. He had often privately informed his mother that he would rather take the most vicious young filly that ever kicked against the bridle, and ride break-neck over fifty miles of cross country, than be forced to hold an argument with cousin Fan, and be snubbed and taken up short by such a little nettle. With these feelings towards the fair lady, it was not in the least remarkable that the rejected knight should make his retreat from the scene of action in such suspicious and undignified haste, or that he should be so well content to hide his diminished head until he could safely assure himself that the heiress had really left town.

George bore his disappointment with an equanimity that was very irritating to his mother, for all that lady's eloquence could not succeed in divesting him of his own private opinion that his cousin had done a kind thing in rejecting him. Still, the recollection of this unfortunate love passage was a source of much mortification to him, and he was ready to resent an allusion to it from any of his brothers as a personal insult.

The young man sat by the window, ruefully watching the splash of the rain-drops in the little pools of water collected in the hollows of the pavement, occasionally diverting the monotony of this occupation, and trying to relieve his mind under the infliction of the maternal lecture, by pulling the ears of a small fat poodle, called Tiny, whom he had taken on his knee, and who lay blinking at him, too lazy even to resent his unpleasant familiarities. He looked up as his sister entered, and, twirling one of Tiny's silken ears over his fingers, whistled softly to himself, secretly pleased at the diversion which this interruption would furnish. Though not the most affectionate of sisters to him, he liked Alice in his own way, and regarded her as a splendid specimen of womankind, or as he phrased it "a real thorough-bred."

"There, ma, do me the favour to read this," exclaimed the young lady, tossing a letter on her mother's knee, and drawing up her graceful figure into an attitude before the mantel glass, for though no eligible bachelor was present to be impressed by the movement, it was excellent practice for future occasions, and Alice Foster always made the most of such opportunities. She watched with a curious kind of interest the varying expression of her mother's face as she read the letter. Perhaps there was a little conscious triumph under all, for events had proved her such an excellent judge of character. She had always predicted Fanny Templeton would inevitably disappoint all the expectations of her friends, and in spite of her wealth, would prove no credit to the family after all. In outward appearance at least, Miss Foster's temper had calmed down to its habitual level. She seemed to gain what her mother lost in composure, for as the elder lady became flushed and excited, the younger smiled to herself, and, glancing almost playfully over her shoulder, condescended to take some gracious notice of her brother, whose presence in the room she had not till then even acknowledged by a look.

Mrs. Foster threw the letter on the table with an expression of vexation and annoyance, and began to rock herself in a quick, irritable manner.

But this did not satisfy her daughter. "Well, ma," she began, in her smiling, provoking way, "What do you think of this precious epistle from the most amiable of nieces and cousins? A very valuable connexion she is, is she not? It will truly be a distinction now to be received into the select circle at Woodlands. Intimate with a dressmaker! To what republican level shall we descend at last? Tell me, ma; you who were daring enough to dream of giving our poor George such a treasure of a wife."

The angry flush deepened on Mrs. Foster's cheek, but her eyes fell beneath that mocking glance. The truth was, that she was a little afraid of her daughter, whose imperious temper always over-ruled hers.

When the much-enduring George heard himself mentioned by his sister in that tone of contemptuous pity, he turned his chair sharply round, and dropping Tiny on the carpet with an abruptness and want of ceremony that was most offensive to the nerves of that much-injured animal, he muttered savagely to himself, "I'm not going to be 'poor Georged' by Ally, as if I was only ten years old. I might take it from the old woman, but I won't stand it from Ally, by Jove, it looks so tame to be ridden over by a girl. The fellows may well laugh at me for being under my sister's thumb and finger." He reddened fiercely at this last consideration, and feeding his newly-kindled anger with every stimulating thought that was likely to add a spark to the flame, he snatched up a book of prints, which he pretended to turn over with an air of careless, gentlemanly ease, that did not sit very naturally upon him. And further excited by the sort of amused surprise with which he saw his movements watched by the two ladies, he desperately resolved to avenge all old insults and humiliations, by flinging down the gauntlet of defiance before his haughty sister. He suddenly startled her by saying, "You may sneer about dressmakers as much as you please, Ally, but I'll stand up for the whole lot, if it's only for the sake of that nice quiet girl that you used to bully so in your high way, and if you mean that she is going to live at Woodlands, all I can say is that it will make the place a deuced deal pleasanter than it ever was before, and I shouldn't mind making friends with cousin Fanny, for the sake of having a fortnight's shooting down there. I can't see that we have so much reason to hold up our heads above dressmakers, for we all know that our great grandfather Foster kept a draper's shop, and it's just as likely that he married a milliner."

All this had been spoken very rapidly. He would not allow himself to breathe freely until he had relieved himself by this (to him) unusually long speech. He had been suffered to proceed without interruption, for profound astonishment had sealed the lips of his mother and sister.

What could be the meaning of this extraordinary exhibition of spirit? It was truly a most remarkable phenomenon that George, the butt of the family wit, and generally the scape-goat for the family sins, that he, above all others, should dare to utter such heretic opinions, and break away from the precepts and prejudices which Mrs. Foster had made part of his education. This last daring allusion to his great grandfather's occupation, a humiliating secret which had always been carefully ignored by the family, fell upon the elder lady with a crushing weight of pain and mortification. The effect upon Miss Foster was characteristic. It stung her into instant self-possession. She went up to her brother, first casting a quick searching glance at the door, as if to satisfy herself that no prying servant had caught his last sacrilegious speech, and stood looking down at him with flashing eyes, her imperial figure drawn up to its full height, and her voice trembling with indignant passion.

"How dare you, George Foster, intrude your opinions unasked, and insult us with your language from the stables? The character of your pursuits, and your well-known taste for low life, might have prepared us for something of the kind. But, that you should dare to speak thus in your father's house. What do you mean by it, sir?"

The young man was startled by this outbreak, and could not help showing it. As he had no answer at command, he singled out a particular flower in the pattern of the carpet and sought inspiration by keeping his eyes steadily fixed upon it. The force of habit was struggling with his fear of looking foolish, and not being able to retain the new ground which he had taken. His sister was so accustomed to exact and receive homage from him. He had always looked up to her with such secret pride in her beauty and high spirit, for which he had exalted her above all other women of his acquaintance. The secret of her power was the rule of a strong mind over a weak one, the dominant sway that a bold decided character can usurp over the mentally feeble and vacillating.

Alice saw her advantage, and unwisely pursued it too far. The tortured fish was already struggling and writhing on the line, but she trifled with it until an unlucky jerk plunged it back to liberty and independence.

"You do not speak, sir. Is it because you are ashamed or sullen? Degenerate boy! I will call you so, for though you have a man's years, you are still a boy in all that is required to take a man's place in the world, and act a man's part."

This was perhaps the only taunt that could

so effectually have roused all the spirit that George possessed, for it touched him where he was most sensitive. The fear of ridicule was one of his strongest feelings, and the word boy was to him a reproach synonymous with everything that was most insulting and degrading.

It sent the angry blood tingling even to the roots of his hair. He ground the heel of his boot fiercely on the carpet, and, turning round, faced his sister boldly. Alice Foster never regained over her brother the influence she lost that morning.

"If you were not a woman, you should repent those words. If a man had said that to me, we should be quits precious soon. He should find that whether boy or man, I could hit out hard and hold my own."

The passionate colour went and came on the cheek of the proud girl. She was as much startled as she was enraged at the way in which her words had been met, but she laughed scornfully, and drew back a step or two, using her scent bottle, as if to remove some offensive odour.

"What! you dare even to be brutal in your coarseness! Do you mistake me for one of the low creatures whom you are in the habit of honouring with your friendship? Or are you acting upon hints received from your amiable cousin, and her friend the dress-maker, in whom you are pleased to take such an interest? I wish I could forget that you are a Foster, for I am positively ashamed of our relationship."

There was an angry retort upon the young man's lips, but it was checked by the voice of his mother, who had now sufficiently recovered her self-possession to interpose in low, deprecating tones,

"George, George, is this the way you repay me for all my anxiety to advance your interests? I could never have anticipated such ungrateful conduct from you. How will you be able to look your sister in the face again after behaving so rudely to her? I must request you to leave the room, sir, until you have recovered your reason and your temper, for you have lost both in a way that I cannot understand." Then seeing her daughter about to speak, she gave her an entreating look, and motioning her to her side, whispered soothingly, "Alice, my dear, you really must not excite yourself so much. Remember you have accepted Mrs. Wilson's invitation for her assembly this evening; but if you agitate yourself in this way I fear you will not be equal to the exertion."

George did not require a second bidding, for he had been longing to leave the room for the last half-hour. He had his hand on the door-knob, when Mrs. Foster said,

"George, I hope you are ashamed of yourself."

He turned, with a flash of sudden fire in his eyes, and answered in a dogged, determined voice, that made her look at him in astonished dismay,

"Ashamed? No! Why should I be? That's always the way with you all. If there's any shame or blame to be thrust on anyone, I'm sure to be the marked card. It's not likely that I'm to stand being insulted as I've been to day, and not say a word for myself. I'm not going to be the tame, spiritless ass that I was when you got me to make an idiot of myself with cousin Fanny, and get laughed at as I deserved. I'm tired of being always in harness, and never having a will of my own; tired of being lectured and sneered at, and looked down upon by you all. Better by half to cut the whole concern, and turn groom, or horse-breaker, or anything, though I am a Foster, which I hold is no great distinction."

It took only a few moments to say all this. It burst from him in a breathless impetuous torrent of words, as if he had a fear of not making the most of the present opportunity of asserting himself. He did not wait to see the effect of his daring speech, but flung himself out of the room, shutting the door after him with a sharp, defiant snap, that sounded to poor, frightened Mrs. Foster, like the death knell of her power over her rebellious son. His last formidable threat about the groom and horse-breaker was still ringing in her bewildered ears, and for once she was natural and sincere. It was a real motherly fear that spoke in her apprehensive look as she said :—

"Alice, did you hear him? I don't know what has come over the boy, he has been moody and sullen for the last few days. I must go after him, and reason with him, before he leaves the house, or he will be doing something desperate."

She would have risen from her seat, but Alice laid her hand on her arm, and forcibly restrained her, saying in a clear cold voice,

"You shall do no such thing, mamma; you shall not yield to such weakness if I can prevent it. Follow him now, and you will confirm him in his exaggerated ideas of his importance, and give him power to tyrannise over you. This is really a new and startling phase of his character, but he must not be allowed to think that it excites any other feeling than contempt. The stream is noisy and shallow, it has broken away from its natural bounds; only wait, and it will fall back to its level."

Mrs. Foster allowed herself to sit passively still, but she glanced nervously towards the door, as she said, dubiously,

"You are quite right, my dear, no doubt; but are you really sure that there is no danger of George doing anything rash?"

"I have told you my opinion, mamma," Alice answered, with a gesture of impatience; "leave him to himself; he has been allowed to occupy too much of our time and thoughts. I protest that this morning's scene has been perfectly disgraceful; as for his insolence to me, the truth is that I feel too much contempt even to take the trouble to resent it, as I should if it came from another source."

She laughed scornfully, to show her perfect indifference to the sayings and doings of an inferior being like her offending brother, but her beautiful face was pale with suppressed passion, and there was a vexed shadow on her brow that contradicted her words.

"Well, mamma, to return to this very interesting letter from Woodlands; I believe you have not yet favoured me with one word of your opinion of my cousin's proceedings?"

Mrs. Foster looked, as she felt, worried, and disposed to be very irritable, if she had not been held in check by some strong counter influence, the old habit of allowing herself to be governed by her handsome and accomplished daughter.

"Why, my dear, I can have but one opinion, that it is a piece of unfeeling impertinence of Fanny to write to us in such a style when she is perfectly aware what view we are likely to take of her conduct. I am very glad that I took your advice about discharging my debt to that dressmaker. If I had never had the misfortune to employ her at all, she would not have been coming to the house, neither she nor her messengers, and all this would have been averted. I can foresee that it will be a serious disadvantage to us, and I shall always reproach myself for want of prudence and discernment. But who would ever have supposed that my patronage of that girl would lead to her being domesticated at Woodlands. It is most extraordinary," continued Mrs. Foster, warming with her subject, and for the time forgetting her own domestic troubles, "How Miss Lomax can countenance her niece in such folly. The idea of taking such a violent fancy to a young person like that Grace Arnold. Taking her from such a low position, out of the streets, I might almost say, and allowing her to be received in the house on such ridiculous terms of equality. I will write myself to Miss Lomax, and try if I cannot reason her into some proper sense of Fanny's—"

"It would be no use, mamma," interrupted

Alice, confidently. "I am sure Miss Lomax is quite as far gone as her niece. Besides, you must remember that Fanny is of age, and therefore legally entitled to take the responsibility of her own actions."

"It is just what might have been expected from a Lomax," commented Mrs. Foster, fretfully; "Fanny always clung most to her mother's family, she never was like the Templetons. Ah! if her father had lived, things would have been different. She would not have been spoiled by her aunt and uncle as she has been all her life. You have often heard me say, Alice, that I never approved of my brother's marriage. He was quite thrown away on Emily Lomax. She was never suited for his wife, and I disliked her family even more than I did herself. Will was the kindest brother in the world before his marriage, but from that time I was quite set aside."

Mrs. Foster folded down the hem of her cambric handkerchief, and threw herself back in her chair with a sigh of sentimental suffering. But though her daughter had preserved an appearance of attention, she had been occupied with her own thoughts, and immediately returned to the subject from which her mother had digressed.

"It is evident from this letter, mamma," she said, taking it slowly from the table, her white, ringed fingers playing nervously with it, as if she had an irresistible inclination to tear it into shreds, and was only restrained by the thought that sometime, perhaps, it might be useful as a reference; "it is evident that our affectionate relative has taken some pains to impress upon us the fact, that this *protegè* of hers (lady's maid, or companion, or whatever they may please to call her) is to be treated with all kindness and respect as one of her most valued friends. I believe I quote exactly her own words. So you see, mamma, our intercourse with Woodlands must end, for, of course, we could not visit there while that person stays. Just fancy us sitting down to dinner with the girl who made our dresses."

Mrs. Foster's assent was somewhat feebly given, for she had private reasons of her own which made this breach with Woodlands a most disagreeable alternative. It involved the sacrifice of the many benefits which they had derived from its richly stored gardens and greenhouses, besides the loss of the Christmas hampers and the liberal presents of game which the state of her housekeeping funds had often converted into a seasonable relief; and then it was so desirable and convenient to have such a house open to them in the summer months. But she knew that her daughter would not stoop to consider anything of this kind. She was revolving in her own mind, whether it would not be possible to make some dignified compromise between pride and interest, when Alice suddenly broke the thread of her musings.

"Mamma, do you recollect a person called Clare?"

"Clare," repeated Mrs. Foster, rousing herself to make the required demand upon her memory, "why, my dear, I confess I am slightly at a loss. Clare? Is that name on our visiting list? Is the person one whom it is desirable to know?"

"I mean old Matthew Clare, the rich stock-broker. Papa knows him. I believe they have been connected in business. He has a nephew."

"A nephew!" interrupted Mrs. Foster, with newly-awakened interest. "Ah, now I remember. He was a tall, dark young man, not exactly handsome, but distinguished looking. We saw a great deal of him at one time, for he was received into very select circles."

Miss Foster slightly smiled an assent.

Her mother continued, "And, my dear, was it not understood that he was to be heir to the old man's wealth?"

"Yes, if he marries to please his uncle. I believe he has no prospects independent of him."

Mrs. Foster mused a moment, then carefully examining her daughter's face, said softly,

"Do you know, my love, I had once a fancy that you two would just suit each other. In fact, I was a little anxious that you should; for, with his expectations, I considered him quite an eligible connexion. To be sure, the uncle is peculiar, and eccentric in his own person, but the nephew is a gentleman in every sense of the word. If I remember right, he went abroad, did he not, rather suddenly on some important business for his uncle?"

Alice was busy with the fastening of her bracelet, but she looked up as her mother ceased speaking, and tightening the clasp round her white arm, until she visibly shrank from the pain, said with a curious smile,

"I believe you are right, ma, but just now that has nothing to do with the reason why I recalled the Clares to your remembrance. I can readily imagine your astonishment when you find me actually coming back to our original topic of conversation—Cousin Fanny's *protegè*, the ex-dressmaker. It is really most extraordinary how that young person has contrived to escape from her proper sphere."

"Grace Arnold?" exclaimed Mrs. Foster, with a puzzled, inquiring air. "My dear, I do not understand what association can possibly exist between her and young Mr. Clare."

"Nor I, either," interjectured the young lady, with a short, bitter laugh. For as the vision of Harry Clare passed before her, surrounded with the luminous halo of future riches, she could not endure the thought that a creature like Grace Arnold should have a claim upon the regard of one for whom she had herself cherished a secret preference. It seemed to presume a sort of equality between them that was wormwood to her haughty spirit.

"Yet so it is," she continued, governing her anger by an effort. "I find that the girl is not only known to Mr. Harry, but that a sort of engagement has actually existed between them for some time."

"Engagement! how perfectly absurd," said Mrs. Foster, almost starting from her seat. "What artful duplicity that creature has practised upon our unsuspecting benevolence. I see now why she was always so reserved in speaking about herself and her family, but I acknowledge myself completely deceived in her. With regard to this silly affair, of course it will never be anything serious. Mr. Harry Clare is not the first young gentleman who has thought it worth while to amuse an idle hour by some nonsense of that kind. I venture to say that he has already forgotten it. When is he expected to return?"

"Some time next month."

"Of course old Mr. Clare will not approve of such a connexion for his nephew."

"No. I believe he has taken some decided measures to break it off. He was mixed up in some way with the account of her father's death. He had some money claim upon that person. A few chance words from Cousin Fanny gave me the clue, but she has learnt to be reserved lately. I suppose she has taken lessons in caution from that crafty old servant of hers. Well, unfortunately we can do nothing but wait and watch the progress of events."

The stopping of a carriage at the door, followed by a loud ring at the bell, here put an end to the conversation.

"It is the Heartleys," exclaimed Alice, "you will be at home to them, of course, mamma. They are not people whom we can afford to slight, but you must make excuses for my absence. I really cannot endure their small tattle this morning."

And crushing Fanny's letter in her hand, the fair lady swept out of the room, leaving her mother to prepare herself to do the honours of reception to the visitors.

## CHAPTER VIII.

The early spring day had been unusually bright and warm. The first of the season which had been welcomed for its happy promise of summer.

The evening was fast closing in with soft grey shadows and light showers of genial rain, which seemed to come down like a blessing on all budding green life, leaving a refreshing coolness and scent in the air that suited well the timid,tender light of the young May moon just visible behind a veil of white feathery clouds, but it was already dark in the dull, silent square where old Matthew Clare lived.

It was always gloomy there on the brightest days, for the tall old houses looked as if they were in mourning for their departed gentility. Mr. Clare's was a large old-fashioned mansion, that seemed to have isolated itself from its neighbours, and stood sullenly back from the rest, looking, in all seasons, solemnly dreary, comfortless, and cold, as if the sunlight had never brightened its heavily curtained windows, and the free fresh air had never been allowed to enter its stately, closed-up rooms. It stood in an enclosed piece of ground, which, by extreme stretch of courtesy, was called a garden, its only pretensions to that title consisting of two weedy patches of unwholesome looking grass on each side of the straight paved walk that led up to the front door, and a dusty-stunted tree in one corner, which had long since desisted from its despairing efforts to clothe itself with green leaves. This domain was presided over by a lean, fierce dog, who shared all his master's aversion to people who bore any signs of poverty in their appearance. He delighted in making sudden vindictive rushes out of his kennel, and growled at the extreme length of his chain whenever a stranger opened the gate. It looked a cold, blighted region. The last place in the world that we could associate with the dear name of home, or where we should expect to hear the sweet prattle of childish voices, or dream of finding any charmed household circle of satisfied loving hearts, or happy, useful, human lives.

The room where the master of the house sat was inconveniently crowded with rich old-fashioned furniture, but it communicated no sense of comfort. It wanted the subtle charm of pure taste, the light relieving touches of grace, and the little intuitive refinements that surround a gentle feminine presence, and attest in so many ways the presiding of a loving woman's hand.

On entering the room the visitor was oppressed with a stifling, uncomfortable feeling, for everything had the same hard uncompromising look, from the heavy folds of its dark window curtains, to the rigid order of the fire-irons and the chilling severity of the gloomy oil painting of Mr. Clare's mother, over the mantel, an inflexible looking, hard eyed old lady, in an antique cap and gown, who seemed to loom weirdly and darkly down upon her son, who looked the living reflection of the picture as he sat in his stiff-backed arm chair, balancing an unwieldy ledger on his knee, the only book that he ever cared to study. His wrinkled hands crossed on the open leaves, and his keen worldly face bent down, with a curious expression of apprehension, mingled with cunning, fox-like watchfulness. It was not the intricate rows of figures that he was so intently reading, but the face of his nephew, who on this, the third evening since his return, was breathlessly awaiting his uncle's answer to his often repeated questions, "Where was Grace Arnold? How was it that he could obtain no knowledge of her present position, and why had she never answered his letters?"

The young man sat opposite to his uncle. The agitating struggles of painfully conflicting feelings were visibly marked in his features. His clear brow was over-cast by some unwonted shadow, and his frank, truthful eyes searched the old man's face with a look of sorrowful questioning eagerness, that would have moved any other less pitiless observer. His age might be twenty-four or five, perhaps a year or two more.

The journey abroad had altered him little beyond giving a duskier hue to his complexion and improving the muscular development of his figure. He could not be called handsome. His face was very far from boasting the regularity of a Greek model. At a first glance it might possibly impress the beholder as unattractive and plain. It was a face that grew into your regard and appreciation, little by little, like a picture studied in new lights. Its greatest charm lay in its power of expression. The features were decidedly irregular, but they had each a distinctive character, that made up an harmonious and singularly attractive whole. The firmness of the mouth, and the decision of the chin were softened and relieved by sensitive, tender lines, not often found in conjunction with such opposite features. But the noble benevolent head was a study in itself. It was a type from which to draw the likeness of a hero, one who would stand by a fallen friend or an unpopular cause, and scorn to shirk a duty from motives of self-interest. You felt that you could rely upon him that what he had to do he would do bravely and well, and that his love would endure to the end, strong, and steadfast and true as steel. This was Harry Clare, to whom Grace Arnold had given all the love of her young heart.

The old man still watched him silently. He had always been proud of his nephew. It was his ambitious hope that the name of Clare would be ennobled in his person, that he would make a brilliant marriage, and be the founder of a family of wealth and distinction. This was the destiny which old Matthew Clare had carved out for his nephew, and to realize which he was prepared to make any sacrifice of principle or conscience. His regard for Harry was a nearer approach to affection than he entertained for any other human being, still it was a modification of selfishness. Through him he ministered to the gratification of his own ruling passions.

It was Harry's voice that broke the long, awkward pause.

"Uncle, this suspense is becoming torture; I feel sure that you can relieve it if you will. In one word, say if you will help me to obtain the information I seek about Miss Arnold, or leave me to place the worst construction on your strange silence."

There was a little uneasy flicker of the old man's eyes, as he slowly transferred them from the face of the speaker to the pages of his ledger. He kept one finger abstractedly fixed on a particular column of figures, as if his mind was intent upon solving some perplexing arithmetical problem, but like a wary general he was in reality reviewing his ground, studying his plan of attack and defence, and debating what line of tactics would be best adapted to his purpose, which was, to subjugate his nephew's will and ensure his obedience without setting the young man's conscientious scruples in array against him or rousing the free independent spirit which he dreaded more than all.

He knew that the time had come when Harry must be made aware of his real intentions respecting him and the plans he had formed for his future. It was no longer possible to keep him in ignorance of the change which circumstances had effected in his past friendly relations with the Arnolds. He had hitherto forborne to cross his nephew's inclinations in that direction, simply because he had clung to the belief that the flame would burn itself out, that time and change of scene would be certain to cure Harry of his boyish folly. He could not believe in love; it was to him purely a fiction something far out of the range of his sympathies—which had no actual existence except in the minds of moon-struck boys and girls and the pages of novels, which he always despised as waste paper. It had no marketable value, it could not be traded upon, there was nothing in it with which he could claim kindred. The beautiful, fervent language of a loving young heart was to him dead and untranslatable as a column of ancient hieroglyphics.

The young man slightly changed his position, shifted his chair so that the full gleam of the shaded lamp fell upon his uncle's face, while he sat more in shadow. Mr. Clare noticed the movement, and affecting to rouse himself by an effort from a fit of abstruse calculation, looked up, with the apparently careless inquiry,

"What were you talking about, Harry?"

His nephew answered with a little deepened colour in his cheek—

"About Miss Arnold, uncle, and your unaccountable evasion of the subject whenever I have attempted to introduce it. You cannot say that I have intruded my affairs upon you at an unseasonable time, when business had a right to engross your attention. I have done my duty as your agent; you have found my accounts punctual and correct, and you have been satisfied concerning the most minute details. Uncle Matthew, you are not using me either justly or kindly, for you know what vital interest I have in the question you seem so unwilling to answer."

Now or never the ice must be broken by a bold decisive plunge. A moment was sufficient for old Matthew to take up his position. He seized at once upon his nephew's last words.

"Vital interest, Harry! I thought that travelling would take all that sentimental stuff out of you. But seriously, my boy, do you wish me to believe that it is a matter of importance to you where that girl—"

"That girl!" Harry interrupted hastily, "whom do you mean, uncle?"

"Grace Arnold, to be sure," the old man replied, with a low, unpleasant laugh, "the dressmaker, or whatever she may be pleased to call herself now, daughter of John Arnold, bankrupt, lately deceased; whom else could I mean, Harry? If you have any more fancies of the same kind you have at least kept them snugly secret. But why did my choice of words offend you?"

Harry's face flushed even to his temples; but when he spoke his manner had not lost any of the habitual respect which he always yielded to his uncle. In strict truth, affection could not be said to have ever made a bond between them; there was nothing in the old man to call out such feelings. He had always repelled, rather than encouraged, such demonstrations from his nephew. All he craved from him was passive, unquestioning obedience, and blind willingness to be made the instrument of his ambition.

Within the last few moments there had been a sudden revulsion in Harry's feelings. Dim undefined fears now shaped themselves into realities. His uncle's last words had given him a key to all that had been suspicious and doubtful in his conduct towards him since his return to England. He could guess all that the old man was preparing to exact from him, and had a prophetic impression that from that evening there would be a jar in their intercourse; and while his mind shadowed out the future struggle that must divide them, he deplored it with a sense of pain that had something almost filial in it. But the after consequence to himself, the probable injury to his own worldly prospects, troubled not his thoughts. Thinking that he had gained an advantage, Mr. Clare repeated his inquiry in the same jeering tone, "Answer me, Harry, are you really angry because I do not pay due respect to your divinity of the needle and thread?"

There was a warning flash in the young man's eyes, that checked him in the full tide of his humour. "Uncle," said Harry's grave, resolute voice, "You have claims on my gratitude that I cannot forget, for though never the most affectionate of relatives, you have been my guardian and protector for many years. This gives you a natural advantage, you are in a degree privileged against retaliation; but there are certain limits beyond which it is unwise to test any kind of power. There are things which no man will tamely endure, unless he is something below a man. I warn you, uncle, that this kind of provocation may force me to forget our relative positions, for I hold it my duty to defend that lady's name from insult. I will have no slight cast upon my future wife, even by you."

"Your wife! sir," the old man exclaimed, in a loud angry voice, losing all self-command in the sudden tempest of passion that shook his wiry, reed-like figure, and glowed under his heavy grey eye-brows. "Your wife!" he repeated fiercely, clutching the arm of his chair, as if he could thus crush down the spirit that opposed his will. "That shall never be, Harry Clare! I would sooner follow you to your grave, and see our family name die out, than have it linked with pauperism and beggary."

The young man calmly rose from his seat, with an indignant, irrepressible scorn quivering on his lips and kindling in his eyes. His feelings were not easily stirred to outward demonstration, for they did not lie upon the surface; their strong under-currents ran deep and calm. But now he was roused. When he spoke, his manner was scarcely less excited than his uncle's.

"My forbearance will not go beyond this, sir. I should despise myself if I could sit here and listen calmly to this most unjust and uncharitable reflection on a family whose undeserved misfortunes will be a sufficient shield of protection to all generous and honourable men. For myself I shall be proud to call Grace Arnold my wife, and consider that she will confer an honour on the man shemarries."

Old Matthew Clare laughed bitterly as he said—

"There spoke the true son of the late Lieutenant Clare, my luckless brother, who had not worldly wit enough to keep a guinea in his pocket, or save himself from getting entangled with the first pretty face that came in his way, and ruining his prospects by marrying a girl without a shilling. These things must run in the blood."

Even in that moment of angry excitement, the allusion to his parents brought a softened expression to the young man's face, as he answered,

"From my own experience of the perfect happiness of that marriage, uncle, I know that my dear mother did honour to my father's choice, even as my Grace will to mine."

"Your Grace. How dare you call her yours?" interrupted the old man savagely.

"Yes, uncle, mine. I recognise no power that can separate us. To win her has been the hope and dream of my life. I would not part with it for all your riches."

"Fool! Idiot! You would throw away your chances in life, sacrifice yourself, and lose all for the sake of that pale-faced girl; but, I say again, it shall never be."

"Who can prevent it?"

"I can, and will."

"You mistake the extent of your power, uncle. I am willing to consult your wishes in anything reasonable and just, but in this you have no right to control me. It is a question in which my dearest interests are involved. Your will shall not come between me and my life's happiness."

"Headstrong, ungrateful boy," retorted the old man, trembling with passion; his unreasoning exasperation increased by the calm resolute tone of his nephew's opposition until he had no longer power to discriminate between what it would be prudent to say, or to leave unsaid. "Is it for this that I took you from your own poor home and poorer prospects, that I passed over the old quarrel with my brother, and for your sake even stooped to make the first friendly advances to his wife, that, through you, the name of Clare might be preserved for wealth and distinction? Is it nothing that I have saved and toiled for years, lived for this one purpose, only to be disappointed where I had a right to expect such a different return? To have you flinging back your obligations, defying me even to my face; and for what—a girl, a mere picture, a toy, the artful scheming daughter of a thriftless, improvident father. She loves you only because your expected fortune will give her back the ease and comfort she has lost."

"It is false, Uncle Clare. You know as well as I that you cruelly wrong one of the truest and noblest natures; but nothing shall shake my faith in Grace Arnold."

"Not, I suppose, if you had positive proof of the worthlessness of your divinity," sneered the old man, inwardly chafing at the thought that all he wanted now was to be able to show his nephew a written renunciation of his addresses by Grace, which he could represent as coming voluntarily from her.

If money could have procured a successful imitation of her handwriting he would have had a letter forged in her name, for he would not hesitate to employ any treachery to obtain the desired end.

Harry smiled in the security of unshaken love and confidence as he said,

"I should be unworthy of Grace if I could not trust her."

"And yet," replied his uncle, "you tell me that she answered none of your letters; but, of course, you take it for granted that all will be explained to your entire satisfaction."

Harry winced with pain at these words. But he answered firmly,

"Yes, I believe she will give me sufficient

reasons for her unaccountable silence. It was most unfortunate that I was called away so suddenly, we could make no arrangements for our correspondence. Are you sure, uncle, that she received all the letters entrusted to your care?"

It was a chance question, for he had not the faintest suspicion of the truth. He had always found his uncle upright and unimpeachable in his business relations, and his own truthful nature could not conceive the idea of such heartless treachery and falsehood; if it had occurred to him it would have been decidedly negatived. But if he had watched the old man's face at that moment, its sudden paleness and terrified startled look might have roused some unpleasant doubts.

A rapid questioning look from the keen grey eyes searched Harry's face suspiciously, but this scrutiny seemed to re-assure him. He breathed freely, for he knew that his secret was safe. He was not betrayed. The subject was too dangerous to himself for him to wish to prolong it. He took refuge in the convenient assumption of offended dignity.

"What, do you doubt my word? Has your love for that girl so far absorbed every other feeling, that for her sake I, your best friend, am to be exposed to such degrading suspicion?"

But though he assumed this high tone of outraged feeling he studiously avoided his nephew's eye, and his mind was filled with secret fear and distrust.

"Uncle, let us end this painful scene at once, and say good night. It will, perhaps, save us much future regret in recalling this night's conversation. I have but one request to make. Will you give me the information I seek about Grace Arnold or leave me to obtain it elsewhere, for I am resolved not to rest until I have found her?"

"I am not Grace Arnold's keeper," returned the old man sullenly. "I know nothing except that her father died in a wretched attic in some low lodging-house, and was buried by strangers who had some loose cash to throw away. And for her, if she is not in service she is living on charity. I can tell you no more."

"Good Heavens!" broke out Harry, pacing the hearth-rug in an agony of feverish agitation, "is it possible that you knew them to be reduced to such extremity, perhaps actually witnessed their distress, yet with all your teeming riches could spare nothing to relieve them. Oh, uncle, I have often heard you called a hard man, but never till now did I believe you inhuman and cruel. You seem to have conceived a strange, sudden aversion to poor, suffering Grace. What can it mean? You once approved my choice; our correspondence was to be conducted through you. You never opposed our engagement before I went to India. How am I to account for this change?"

"Blind, infatuated boy! The reason would be obvious to any one else. When you first engaged yourself, it was to the daughter of a prosperous merchant, not a ruined bankrupt. I allowed your acquaintance to go on, after her father's failure because I was a doting, self-deceived, old idiot, and did not dream that you had then any serious intentions about the girl, or meant anything except to amuse yourself like the rest of young men."

"What! did you mistake me so far, as to judge me base enough to find amusement in trampling out the happiness of a human life and trifling with a woman's priceless love, a woman like my Grace? No, sir! If I was the sordid, despicable earth-worm that your words have hinted, I would be crushed out of existence and rid mankind of a disgrace to their humanity."

"Miserable, reckless young man, you will live to repent this; like other fools, you will wake from your dream of folly and find your idol only a piece of common clay. You prized her for her beauty, I tell you she has lost it; I saw her changed and faded."

As he said this he looked into his nephew's

face, his eyes lighting up with a fierce exulting gleam.

"I care not, uncle; I love Grace Arnold for something more precious and enduring than physical beauty—her true heart and noble soul!"

The ledger fell on the carpet with a dull, heavy sound, and the old, hard face grew livid, even to the thin crafty lips.

"Then this is your decision, boy! In defiance of my wishes, you intend to seek that creature and marry her?"

"Yes, uncle, now that her father is dead, Grace is more than ever in need of a protector."

"Stuff, you have no means to support a wife, unless you intend to take her to a cottage and live on love and dew."

"I will make her a home by my own honest exertion," said Harry, proudly. "If a man is willing to labour and use the faculties that God has given him he need not ask how he is to live. I do not fear the future."

"Fine talk, no doubt, sir, pity that it has the great fault of being quite impracticable, high sounding words with nothing in them. I should like to see you fighting with the world, you are made of the wrong sort of stuff; but I suppose you mean to go forth like a conquering knight in a romance, and cover yourself with riches and honours. I tell you again that you will repent this folly, you are miserably deceiving yourself. A little rough reality will soon wash the fine colours out of the picture; you will come to your senses in a fit of disgust, to find yourself clogged with a penniless wife, and wonder what you saw in her to be worth the sacrifice you made. It will be the old story again, a poor man's life worn out in mean shifts and disappointed struggles, with nothing to look for at last but a parish coffin and a narrow, unhonoured nook of ground in an obscure corner of some church yard."

Harry contemplated his uncle with a kind of softened pity in his looks. After all, he was his father's only brother, the sole surviving relative of his name and race, the only being in the world who had any natural obligation to be interested in his fate. He could not forget that the crabbed, cross-grained old man had been kind to him, as he had been to none else. That exceptions had always been made in his favour, and that he alone permitted to pass beyond the barrier that excluded the rest of humanity, and suffered to approach the closed, frost bound heart.

Determined will and unshaken purpose could be read in every line of the young man's face. His voice had a clear, courageous ring that could only have been given by a brave, self-reliant spirit, strong in the consciousness of its own well-measured powers, but it took a gentler tone as he said,

"You draw a sad picture, uncle, but it does not discourage me. I would rather take the hard chances of the poor man's lot than waste the best years of my life in aimless idleness, living on rich expectations, bought at the price of my independence of will and action. I could not wear such chains even if I had no stronger motive to break them than mere love of freedom. I consider any drudgery more honourable than this kind of bondage."

"Very good, sir," returned the old man, bitterly. "You have chosen your course, so have I, but mark me, Harry Clare, the day that sees you the husband of Grace Arnold, cuts you off from all hope of assistance from me. From that time you will be my nephew only in name. Not a shilling of my money shall ever be yours. I will leave it to some asylum for idiots. Do you hear, sir? in future we shall be as strangers."

Harry was preparing to retire for the night. He paused near the old man's chair, and with the softened, regretful look in his eyes, held out his hand with a respectful but grave "Good night, uncle. I accept your decision, without questioning either its kindness or its justice, for I know it would be impossible for me to retain my present position on your conditions. To-morrow opens for me a new page in life. It will give me a new home and a new sphere of interest and exertion. I am going to try to do a man's work, among men; but I am sorry this has come between us, uncle, that we are to part as strangers. You have spoken harshly, bitterly, to-night, but my father was your brother. I forgive you."

His proffered hand was sternly thrust aside. The old man drew his own away with a hasty, irritable gesture, and pushed back his chair, saying:

"I do not want your forgiveness, boy. Why should I? You are the offender."

"You do not care for it now, uncle, but some time perhaps you will like to remember that I did not leave you in anger or bitterness of spirit. I do not regret the loss of your fortune—no, not an atom; nor do I quarrel with your decision in favour of the Asylum for

Idiots. It is, I doubt not, an excellent and useful institution. But I hope you will live long to enjoy your wealth before its reversion."

As Harry turned away, his uncle's eyes furtively followed the commanding figure, and clear, well-cut profile. He could not repress a certain feeling of admiration, even in the midst of his own rage and disappointment. Harry Clare was what he looked—a fine, unselfish, noble-hearted fellow, one of those who make the world better and purer by their lives.

Old Matthew rose hurriedly from his seat, and looked eagerly after his nephew, as if he had some further remonstrance to urge upon him, and wished him to stay. But he seemed to re-consider his intention, for without a word he sank heavily back in his chair; and Harry, with a repeated good night, to which no answer was returned, went out, shutting the door gently after him.

The uncle listened gloomily to his nephew's retreating footsteps, then poked the fire fiercely, and drawing his chair up to the fender, spread his wrinkled hands shiveringly over the feeble flame which his energetic application of the poker had evoked from the expiring embers. He rang the bell sharply, ordered in a fresh supply of coal, and mixed himself a double quantity of brandy and water; and when the little, thin, shrewish-looking old housekeeper ventured a modest hint about the lateness of the hour, he quenched even that privileged person with a snarling command that she would go to bed and interrupt him no more. She withdrew in offended silence, concluding that master must be losing money, or that something had gone wrong with Mr. Harry, which reflections she applied as sedatives to her own outraged dignity.

The old man sat there till the dark dreary square was still as the grave and long after all waking sounds were hushed in his gloomy old house. It was getting far into the night when he rose and lighted a chamber candle, listened cautiously at the door for a moment, then stole stealthily up stairs to his own room. He returned after a few minutes' absence, with the same noiseless gliding step, and shutting the door carefully after him, laid on the table a small packet of letters tied together with a piece of red twine. These were the letters which Harry Clare had written to Grace Arnold, and so unsuspectingly confided to his uncle's care. There was an ireful glitter in the old man's eyes as he cut the string, and sorted them out severally, beginning with the one dated from Liverpool, which Harry had hastily written, and posted before he sailed. His uncle did not read the letters, only glanced wrathfully at their date, and the name on the envelopes, muttering under his breath, "He is mad, infatuated; I have mistaken his character all through. If that girl had only died when she was ill with the fever all would have ended well. I disliked her always, but now I hate her."

One by one he threw the letters on the glowing embers, seeming to take a vindictive pleasure in watching the flame leap up, and curl greedily round each paper in succession. "Perish all such miserable folly," he said, in a hissing whisper. "It was unbusiness like to keep them till now, they might have brought mischief."

So he stood feeding the fire with the tender love-words that would have satisfied the pining hunger of poor Grace's heart in her weary time of trial, and would have been hoarded by her as sacred treasures. He watched them shrivel into little heaps of white ashes, which he stirred carefully into the fire, until no vestige remained of his midnight occupation.

Harry did not see his uncle, before he went out next morning, but he found on the breakfast table a sealed note addressed to him in his well-known hand-writing. It contained these words:—

"Still having your future interest at heart, I give you one month to re-consider the rash step you have resolved upon. At the end of that time, if you are still obstinately bent on your own ruin, I give you up, and leave you to reap as you have sown. But I warn you that Grace Arnold is not worth half such costly sacrifices. Whatever her former feelings may have been, I know that she does not care for you now. She told me that she did not wish to keep you to your engagement; that, as far as she was concerned, you were free. Go to her as a poor man, without prospects, and take my word she will throw you over for the first man of more substantial means who may be fool enough to make her an offer."

If Matthew Clare had been watching his nephew he would have been pleased to see the pained quivering of his lips and the sudden deathly paleness of his face. But the result would have disappointed him, for Harry crushed the note in his hand and threw it into the fire, unconsciously consigning it to the same fate which his own had met with on the previous night. But the envenomed arrow had stung him, and some of its poison was still left.

"Oh Grace, Grace!" he moaned to himself, "there is some painful mystery here. Why can I not find her, to vindicate herself? No, I cannot, I will not believe one word unless I hear it confirmed by her own lips. Grace Arnold false, fickle, worldly, selfish. If she is so changed, Heaven pity me. It will take away my trust and uproot my faith in human nature. For me there will be no goodness left in the world, no truth in woman."

## CHAPTER IX.

A DELIGHTFULLY picturesque, old-fashioned country house, with quaint, pointed gables, and a multitude of bright windows that the sunlight seemed to love, it stood on rising ground, commanding from every view a wide stretch of sweet pastoral English scenery. Woodlands was truly a pleasant place to visit at all seasons. It had been the home of the Lomax family for a period that extended far beyond the memory even of that proverbial chronicler of time—the oldest inhabitant of the village. When Fanny's bachelor uncle came back from India, where he had spent the best years of his life, and accumulated his large fortune, it was feared that Woodlands would be abandoned for a residence of more ambitious pretensions, but good, eccentric old Lomax meant nothing of the kind. He settled quietly down in the old house with his maiden sister and his orphan niece, to the great satisfaction of the tenant farmers, and the joy of all the poor in the district.

The morning was deliciously bright and warm, and the little sunny parlour which Fanny called her pet room, and which her fond old uncle had altered expressly to her taste, now wore its most inviting aspect. The long, low window overlooking the pleasantest part of the garden, was open, letting in a burst of sunshine, and a fragrant shower of rose-leaves, shaken from a truant, trailing bush that would push itself intrusively into the room. But the charm of the picture was the striking little group who had just arranged themselves in working order round a small work-table.

First, a pale, gentle-looking, elderly lady, with soft bands of silver hair folded under her neat cap-border, a mouth tender rather than firm, but the kindest smile, the mildest blue eyes, and the most loveable household face that you could hope to meet with in the span of a lifetime. This was Fanny's beloved Aunt Margaret, whose kindly nature was sufficient to redeem the whole generation of old maids from much of the slander cast upon them. She had none of the sharp angles in her figure, nor the vinegar aspect and acidity of temper, generally attributed to that much maligned class.

Opposite sat a tall, slight girl, busily employed with some light needle work. From the clear, well-defined profile, pale, pure face, and eyes so beautiful in their changing lights and soft brown depths of shadow, there was no mistaking her identity. It was Grace Arnold. She had so far recovered from her illness that Dr. Marsh professed to have quite released her from medical discipline. She often smilingly insisted, that as she was no longer an invalid she had no right to be so tenderly nursed and cared for as she was at Woodlands. Yet still she did not get strong. Spring ripened into summer, but the long, bright days found her still frail and languid. There was a depression of spirits, a care-worn, weary look, and a general debility that made Dr. Marsh shake his head, and look grave to Aunt Margaret; and it was doubtless the principal cause of their sudden removal to the sea-side, which was settled to take place early in the following week.

Fanny had a most ostentatious display of needle work before her which did not seem destined to make much progress, as she seemed to find it impossible to sit still more than five minutes together. She would be hanging over Aunt Margaret's chair, or hovering about Grace, doing nothing, with such charming attraction in her idleness, her black eyes dancing in their own light, and her mouth curved into such bewildering dimples. A bright, sparkling, wilful sprite, who could at pleasure make herself either loved or feared, to which last feeling poor George Foster could have borne eloquent testimony.

"So it is all settled," began Fanny, hopelessly entangling a skein of silk. "We are positively to go next week; what a delightful change it will be."

"Yet Woodlands is so very beautiful," Grace murmured softly. "It is such a sweet, peaceful home I wonder you can wish to leave it, dear Miss Templeton."

Fanny poutingly replied, half jesting and half earnest, "Grace, how can you be so obstinate on this one point, and give me so much trouble when you are so good in everything else? I have told you so often that I will not be called Miss Templeton. I hate such ceremony between friends; it sounds as if they were secretly displeased with each other, and trying not to show it. So, remember, Grace, I will be nothing but Fanny to you. What were you saying about Woodlands? To be sure, I agree with you it is a dear old place, so pleasant to come back to when the roving fit is over. Grace, can you think of the sea without becoming enthusiastic? The long, delicious rambles, and the exciting, breezy rides on the sands? Come, Grace, you look pale and sad this morning, throw aside that tiresome work, dear, and I will fetch my guitar and sing your favorite song.

Grace smiled an assent, and answering Aunt Margaret's look of solicitude, acknowledged that she did feel a little out of spirits.

Fanny had returned with her guitar, and Grace was helping to adjust the blue ribbon over her shoulder when Aunt Margaret was summoned to see a poor woman from the village. She had just left the room for this charitable purpose when the sound of carriage wheels on the gravel was followed by a loud ring of the bell, and the almost simultaneous appearance of Dr. Marsh and his nephew, Mr. Cecil Lee.

Fanny Templeton was just sounding the

prelude to her song. It was one that Grace loved for its association with Harry Clare, and the past days of unclouded love and happiness. She sat with her face turned away from Fanny, the darkly fringed lids drooping over her eyes, her whole attitude one of hushed expectation.

The soft plaintive notes were filling the room with sweet sounds when the opening of the door abruptly broke the spell and arrested the hand of the musician, who was discovered by the gentlemen in a state of blushing confusion, most unusual with her, trying to release herself from the ribbon of the guitar, which had become provokingly entangled in her watch chain; for no other reason, she afterwards told Grace in confidence, than because that tiresome Cecil Lee was there.

The doctor made his elaborate old-fashioned bow to the young ladies, then smiling and rubbing his hands went up to his old favourite, and with eyes twinkling with suppressed fun made her a gallant offer of his services in arranging the refractory ribbon, a privilege which perhaps his nephew would have been inclined to dispute with him.

But Fanny saucily refused his aid, which the patient fingers of Grace had made unnecessary. The doctor accused her of despising his services, affected anger, and threatened to be revenged the next time she was ill.

She answered with a provoking smile,

"I don't care, doctor; fore-warned is forearmed, you know, and I intend to keep in such vulgar good health that I shall be independent of the entire medical staff."

Dr. Marsh shook his head, owned that he had no small shot to return for the enemy's fire, and called a truce of hostilities.

"Take care, Miss Fanny; if I was as young as Cecil, you would not come off with flying colours, I can tell you."

"Now, doctor, that is ungrateful, for you know that I am your right hand counsellor whenever you are going to do anything sensible."

"Only hear her," exclaimed the old gentleman, flourishing his silk handkerchief over his shining bald head and passing it across his mouth to hide the broad indications of a laugh, for these little altercations with Fanny always gave him intense delight. "Who would get married, and throw himself into a wasp's nest of his own free will? I am thankful for my escape. Cecil, my boy, I shall expect you to take the warning to yourself."

And he gave his nephew a comical glance that concealed much conscious pride. Now the good doctor's strongly, marked partiality and pride in his nephew, though sometimes amusing, from his efforts to disguise it in an affectation of severity, was most indulgently regarded by the few who knew Cecil Lee well enough to appreciate his fine qualities of mind and heart. The metal was sterling, and had the true ring. He was just the sort of young man to win the heart of a whimsical old uncle who had outlived all other kindred ties. Yet

Cecil was not generally popular; he froze in an uncongenial atmosphere, and could not make himself all things to all men. He was not quickly impressionable, not easily influenced or drawn out. Thus young ladies, who began by making him their hero, ended by voting him an insensible block of marble, and giving him up in hopeless disgust. But most of his fair enemies agreed that he was a decidedly eligible connexion, for he would inherit his uncle's wealth, and he was an artist of acknowledged talent.

From his boyhood, Cecil Lee had been a welcome visitor at Woodlands. He was always a favourite with uncle Lomax, who had often declared in confidence to aunt Margaret, that if he was ever tempted to turn match maker, it would be to bring about an alliance between little Fan and the nephew of his old friend.

And Fanny liked the handsome artist after her own wilful fashion, though she took some pains to conceal it from him. But she knew that Cecil loved her. There had been moments when she had seen flashes from the hidden soul in his deep, calm eyes, and felt his hand tremble as it touched hers in the common interchange of friendly courtesies. Still they met and parted, day after day, and Cecil seemed to find himself no nearer the star he worshipped.

By some means the old doctor had discovered his nephew's secret, and he often made it the subject of a little characteristic raillery.

"I pity you, Cecil. Why did you fall in love with that little witch at Woodlands? To be sure I always liked the midge, and I think I may be brought to give my consent if you ask for it; but the point is, how to catch her, and keep her when she is caught. It will be like trying to cage a sunbeam; but whatever comes of it, my boy, don't say I didn't warn you."

Dr. Marsh had given a very embarrassing turn to the conversation.

Cecil coloured, and glanced uneasily at

the mischievous, smiling Fanny, who was visibly enjoying his uncle's joke. The merciless doctor would have pursued this vein of raillery still further, but luckily for Cecil some well-timed remark from Grace Arnold seasonably diverted his attention. They were soon chatting pleasantly together, the doctor trying to engage Grace in animated talk, and at the same time watching her with careful professional scrutiny, for he had deeper fears for the gentle girl than he was willing to confess even to his old friend aunt Margaret.

By way of recovering his self-possession, Cecil seized a book of drawings, with which he affected to become entirely absorbed, apparently unconscious that his movements were closely watched by a certain pair of inquisitive black eyes.

"Mr. Lee," whispered a gay, well known voice, that sent a glad thrill to his heart, "I hope you will remember the sage maxim which I quoted just now, 'Fore-warned, forearmed;' for with such advice to fortify you against temptation and danger, your friends will have a right to expect from you extra-ordinary results of wisdom and—"

"Miss Templeton," interrupted Cecil, with an impetuosity of manner quite new to him, "tell me, do you include yourself among those kindly interested friends?"

He received a provoking side glance from the arch laughing eyes, as she replied,

"Certainly, sir. I hope I have done nothing to forfeit my right to do so?"

Wilful, tormenting, but always irresistibly fascinating in her changing humours, what power she had to move the usually calm, thoughtful, undemonstrative Cecil. It was in the sudden impulse of that moment that he formed the resolution which was to influence his whole after life. He would speak to her before she left Woodlands and tell her the cherished secret, which she must have suspected long before. Yes, he would try his fate before some bolder rival bore away the long-coveted prize.

"Miss Templeton,—"

"Mr. Lee," she rejoined, quickly interrupting him with one of her low musical laughs.

"Why do you laugh?" he asked, with a touch of disappointment and pain in his voice, sensitively shrinking within himself, as he was wont to do.

"Because it strikes me that you and I are getting upon stilts, which is such an absurd proceeding for two old friends. We used to be natural and content ourselves with christian names, but now we are growing older and seeing more of the world we cannot tolerate such familiarity."

Cecil's grave face brightened; he answered eagerly, "Then let us do our best to repair this error. Suffer me to hope that you will be always Fanny to me—"

He paused abruptly. Fanny remained demurely silent. She had taken a rose from one of the flower vases, and was industriously stripping off its beautiful petals, the long drooping lashes softly veiling her eyes, and a shy, questioning, half startled look on her face. Some unerring womanly instinct told her what revelation was coming.

He began in a trembling, agitated voice,

"Fanny, hear me for a moment. I know this is not the fitting time and place to say what I must no longer leave unsaid if I wish life to be endurable to me. Yes, even at the risk of offending you, I—"

But here the entrance of Aunt Margaret abruptly cut short the interesting sentence, and, for that morning at least, frustrated the lover's hopes.

She came in, with her soft, almost youthful step, smiling on the visitors in kindly recognition, happily unconscious of the cruel disappointment she was inflicting on her favourite Cecil. It was the first time that the young man had ever found the dear old lady's presence unwelcome.

Fanny slipped from his side, and was soon delighting the doctor with her sparkling wit and quick repartees. A new spirit of gaiety seemed to have seized her. Her manner was restless and excited, there was a brighter light in her eyes, and a deeper colour on her clear cheek. But she carefully shunned Cecil's gaze, and pointedly avoided addressing any remark to him.

The visit was prolonged for another half-hour, when the doctor drew out his large old-fashioned watch, seemed incredulous at the flight of time, and jocosely protested that some spirit of mischief must have been tampering with his faithful time-keeper. No hospitable persuasion could prevail upon the gentlemen to stay for lunch.

At the moment of leave taking, Cecil seized the opportunity for which he had been waiting, and whispered hurriedly to Fanny,

"To prove that I have not offended you by presuming too far, will you walk with me in the grounds this evening?"

She blushed, and hesitated.

"Will you, Fanny? Yes or No." Cecil repeated, his lips quivering with excitement.

There was so much of the heart's earnest purpose in his face that the spoiled pet of Woodlands must have felt a secret womanly consciousness that it was no moment for coquetry.

A low, half-timid "Yes," sent Cecil Lee from her presence that morning in such a pleased flutter of lover-like excitement that he more than once exposed himself to his uncle's good-humoured irony during their drive.

"Fanny," said Aunt Margaret, when they were again quietly seated round their work table, "did Cecil tell you how the picture was progressing?" This was one which he was painting for the dinning-room at Woodlands. "I am growing quite impatient."

"That's right, Aunty, I am glad to find that you share some of the foibles of erring humanity, it seems to bring you nearer to us. But about our picture, no, Cecil did not even mention it. Aunt Maggie, Grace, I tell you both, in strict confidence, that I have an impression that the artist is growing shamefully indolent and negligent of his duty. His uncle's indulgence has spoiled him, and he has been over rated and over praised by his friends."

Grace raised her expressive brown eyes, and smiled softly, at which Fanny blushed without any apparent reason.

"Why, my dear, I always thought that you admired Cecil Lee," said simple-minded Aunt Margaret, all unlearned in the mysterious little caprices of love and lovers.

But a timely interruption spared Fanny the embarrassment of replying to this home question, for at that moment the footman handed in a letter for Miss Arnold, with the information that it had been sent by a special messenger from the village postmaster, as it had been overlooked in the early morning delivery of letters.

Grace received it in a little tremor of agitation, with a secret, kindling hope, that sent a vivid colour to her cheek, but it faded as she glanced at the address on the envelope. Her heart sickened with foreboding dread, for she had sad cause to remember that hand writing. The letter was from old Matthew Clare, her father's persecutor and her own. With trembling hands she tore it open, and read,

"GRACE ARNOLD,

"It is needless to allude to the unhappy occasion of our last meeting; it was unfortunate in all its results, and only served to deepen unfavorable impressions on both sides. I know that you dislike me, for in that interview you made no secret of the feeling. If I was inclined to be vindictive, I might take revenge now. But I wish to be your friend, and show you that I take an interest in your welfare, for which I know you will not be disposed to give me credit. I have put myself to some trouble in procuring your address, for I wish to give you a friendly warning. My nephew has returned to England. I have only to say that what I once hinted to you about his altered feelings towards yourself is now confirmed beyond a doubt. But I have reason to suspect that he will attempt to intrude upon your retirement—perhaps even seek to renew his former intimacy. But do not delude yourself with the thought that he is prompted by any affection for you. It would be because he resents your fancied indifference, and seeks only a triumph for his vanity. You will believe this when I tell you he has formed an engagement with the daughter of my former partner, a young lady whose prospects are even better than his own. It is to save you from further pain and mortification that I write to put you on your guard. Some day, perhaps, you will thank me.

"MATTHEW CLARE."

Grace sat very still, gazing at the letter with fixed tearless eyes and white set lips. She had resigned herself to give up the love of her youth, schooled herself, as she believed, to accept her destiny without a murmur, and think of Harry Clare as one who could have no part in her future. But that letter had betrayed the almost unconscious self-deception. It was a re-opening of all the old wounds; she was living over again the bitter time of trial which had over-shadowed her young life.

Fanny gently took the passive, unresisting hands, and softly whispered, "Grace, dear Grace, whatever this new sorrow may be, do not bear it alone, it will make you ill again; let me share it."

And gentle, pitying Aunt Margaret stole to the poor girl's side, and laid her cool, soft hand upon her forehead, saying,

"My poor, poor child! can we help you in any way?"

This was all she said; but the gentle touch and the kind, motherly voice had a healing power of their own, that touched the wounded heart. The rigid lips relaxed, the eye-lids quivered and drooped, and covering her face with her hands, tears fell like rain through her slender fingers.

Fanny passed her arm round her neck, and with a tender, caressing movement, drew the brown head upon her shoulder. Grace wept on for some minutes. Tears seemed a merciful relief to her full heart. When she had recovered calmness, she put the letter into Fanny's hand, saying,

"It comes from old Mr. Clare; you will understand it, for you know my painful history. Read it, dear, then give it to your aunt."

Fanny's black eyes seemed to absorb its contents in one sweeping, scathing glance. When she handed it to her aunt there was fire on her cheeks and in her eyes, flashing through fast gathering tears. Her whole manner was an indignant protest against the letter and its writer.

"Grace!" she cried, with a characteristic burst of impetuous feeling, "that old man is a dishonour to his grey hairs. I should like to torture him where he is most vulnerable, bleed him through his gold; make him distribute to the poor the wealth he has hoarded in selfish avarice. Dear Grace, believe no statement of his. I would not convict a felon on his evidence. His cunning defeats itself. There is treachery and falsehood in every sentence of his letter."

A faint touch of colour drifted into the pale face of Grace, as she answered eagerly,

"Oh! if I could be sure of this. Tell me, dear Fanny, you do not form your estimate of Harry Clare's character from this letter."

"Most certainly I do not, Grace. I am disposed to think much better of him. You would never have loved that old man's nephew if there had not been something worthy of love in him. If I hear of him being in the neighbourhood, or if we chance to meet him anywhere, I will get Aunt Margaret to invite him. You must give him the meeting,

Grace, it is only just that he should have a chance of vindicating himself; and be careful to preserve that letter, it may be wanted, for take my word, dear, old Matthew Clare has some cause for dreading your meeting with his nephew, so he has written to prevent you seeing him; but the old spider shall be caught in his own web. So take heart, Grace; and remember that you are not the first pair of lovers who have passed through great tribulation."

Grace smiled and blushed.

"Thanks, dearest Fanny, your words give me hope, it is such agony to doubt those we have loved and trusted."

Aunt Margaret silently handed back the letter, but her tender, wistful look was more eloquent than words.

Grace held her hand and pressed it warmly, murmuring,

"Dear, kind friends, I owe to your goodness all that makes life worth having."

But here Fanny hastily interrupted her, and assuming a playful tone, exerted herself, not unsuccessfully, to turn the current of poor Grace's thoughts into a less painful channel.

## CHAPTER X.

A GAY party of young men had just emerged from a fashionable club house. One of them, who had obstinately resisted the invitation of his companions to join them in some pleasure excursion, thereby exposing himself to their laughter and ridicule, was left standing at the door alone, moodily smoking a cigar, and watching the heavy gathering clouds that threatened a coming storm. He stood thus until large drops of rain sprinkled the pavement, and a warning peal of thunder broke the unnatural stillness of the breezeless sultry afternoon.

"Ah, I thought we should have it before long," he muttered slowly, puffing away a thin cloud of smoke; "I didn't want to go with those fellows, and now I'm glad I stood out; it showed pluck. I may as well turn in again and finish my cigar on the sofa. It will help me to collect my thoughts, as they say in novels."

At that moment his attention was arrested by a gentleman crossing from the opposite side of the street.

"I think I should know the cut of that face. Well, I'm blessed if it ain't Clare. I'm in luck to-day."

The individual thus apostrophized was in evident haste, and would have passed him without recognition, but the cigar smoker rushed forward, and forcibly intercepted him by the coat sleeve, exclaiming,

"Halloo, Clare! you're not going to give me the cut like this. Haven't you a word for an old friend?"

"Bless me! George Foster! how are you,

my dear fellow? I did not see you, upon my word."

And the other held out his hand with good-humoured cordiality.

"Just come in here, Harry, we can't talk in the street, for if we stand here any longer, by Jove, we shall be in for a shower bath."

Harry Clare hesitated for a moment, stifled a little sigh of impatience, and looked wistfully at the black sky. But a vivid flash of lightning and a loud peal of thunder at once decided the question in George Foster's favour.

He soon found himself in a comfortably furnished room, cosily seated opposite to George, who had ordered in a bottle of wine, and insisted on doing the honours of hospitality, and regardless of Harry's temperate scruples celebrated their chance meeting by enthusiastically drinking his health. Then lighting a fresh cigar, he settled himself in an easy chair, and showed a decided disposition to make what he called a jolly afternoon of it.

Harry Clare had a benevolent wish to adapt himself to his companion's humour, for the young man had shown such genuine pleasure at meeting him. So they talked and laughed, dipped lightly into the current topics of the day, and George, in a high state of pleased excitement, favoured his friend with the newest sporting anecdotes, copiously flavoured with some professional jokes, which might have passed for wit in his own circle.

"Come, Clare, fill your glass, I can recommend this old port. It's the right sort, for our fellows are deuced good judges of wine. Here's to the juice of the grape, Harry, nothing like it, take my word, for warming a man's heart and keeping up his pluck."

"False and dangerous doctrine, my dear fellow; you will find that it carries its own condemnation; seriously, George—"

But George hastily interrupted, giving his mouth a comically dissenting twist,

"All right, Harry; but let us cut the serious for once, and laugh while we may.

Come, old fellow, don't begin to sermonise, if you like me, for your talk always gets beyond me, I can't follow you without getting out of my depth. I should just as soon think of putting that new mare of mine to a fence I know she can't take, or matching her with Dick Walton's thoroughbred chestnut. Fact is, Clare, mother Nature meant you for a parson, I always said you would be a credit to the cloth; rather curious that I could never make out my own vocation. The governor says I am fit for nothing, that he can discover, except to waste money. Well, it's no use disputing the point, I suppose the upshot will be much the same at the end of the race. By the bye, Harry, is it true that you and the old one have had a regular tiff about some love affair of yours, and in short, that—"

"That I have left my uncle; yes, it is true," interrupted Harry, quietly finishing the sentence, his brow flushing slightly, and a shade of perceptible annoyance in his manner, for his feelings were very sensitive on that subject. But he recovered himself as he continued, "Yes, Foster, I am no longer a man of leisure, my time is not my own (at least not for a large portion of the day), for I have just entered upon the duties of my new situation, a banker's clerk ; you will say it is not an ambitious beginning of the world, still it is the first insertion of the wedge. I have tasted the sweets of independence and honourable labour, and I do not regret the step I have taken."

"That's what I call plucky. By Jove you're a regular brick, Harry, and if there is a love affair at the bottom of it, I honour you for standing by the girl of your choice in spite of the old growler and his money-bags; you would not let yourself be sold in the matrimonial market. Tell you what, Clare, you're a trump card. I always liked you at school, for you wern't a sneak, and you never told tales, and bullied the little boys."

"Thanks, thanks, for your good opinion, my

dear fellow," said Harry, laughing at this characteristic estimate of his virtues.

Poor George tried to join in the laugh, but failed in the attempt. He fidgetted restlessly in his chair, trifled nervously with his watch chain, and looked wistfully at Harry. It was clear that there was something on his mind. Harry noticed these unusual signs of mental agitation, and charitably came to the rescue.

"What is it, George? Something has disturbed you; I do not ask from any idle curiosity, but a friendly wish to serve you if I can."

The young man's face flushed as he answered,

"On my soul I believe you, Harry."

He spoke rapidly, crowding his words breathlessly upon each other, as he always did under the influence of excitement.

"I know I'm not one of your sort, Clare; you're a great way above me in everything, that's why I always feel that I can say to you what I could'nt say to any one in my own set ; they would only laugh at me. Well, Harry, to let you into a secret, I'm often deuced dissatisfied with myself and my way of life. I can't see that I'm any use in the world; nothing depends upon me. I have no purpose to live for. I don't know one that wouldn't get on quite as well if I was dead. But I've felt this most when I've seen my poor old governor come home from the city, tired and wearied about money matters, when mother and Ally have been out at parties, and there's not been a soul in the house that he could tell his cares to—for it's true, Harry, the weight is all on his shoulders; and he hasn't a grain of comfort from any of us. It's then that I feel ashamed of myself, and want to be something different to what I am, but it's no use."

And with a desperate, despairing sort of resignation, George relighted his cigar, and poured himself out another glass of wine.

Harry replied, with grave earnestness,

"These feelings do you honour, George.

It depends upon yourself, whether they will bear fruit in actions, for a man is what he makes himself."

He saw a gleam of something like the spirit he wished to kindle brightening in the young man's eyes as he answered eagerly,

"If I could only see you oftener, Clare, I believe it would be the making of me, for I've always better thoughts when I've been with you. But I say, Harry, it strikes me as a noble thing for a man to love a girl for herself, and have pluck to go against the world and take her, though she mayn't be worth a shilling; but when he gives up his chance fortune, rather than lose her, and prefers to work for his bread, why, that must be the true sort of love we see so seldom anywhere out of books. Now I've made up my mind never to marry for money; I have seen so much of it that I'm sick of the whole farce. They wanted to make up a match between me and my rich cousin, Fanny Templeton, not because we're fit for each other, for we're as opposite as the poles; but she was old Brian Lomax's heiress, that's why my mother set her heart on the match, not because she had any liking for the girl herself, I have found that out since. Well, to please the old lady and save myself from being worried, I was fool enough to be put in leading strings, and made a noodle of. I don't mind telling you, Harry, between ourselves; I did actually make my cousin Fan an offer when she was staying with us last winter; but she put out her prickles like a little nettle as she is, and sent me to the right about in such a way that I shouldn't like to repeat the experiment; but at the same time, I thank her, for we should never have got on well together, though I like her as a cousin, for there's no nonsense about Fanny Templeton. She is a sensible girl, and a kind one, too, whatever my sister Ally may say to the contrary. I shall always think well of her, if it's for nothing but taking pity on that poor dressmaker that they're all crying out against. Ah, my dear fellow, to let you into a little secret of my own, that pretty dressmaker was the sort of girl I could fancy likely to inspire a man to brave anything for her sake.'"

"Why, Foster," said Harry, good humouredly forcing himself to be interested, "I begin to suspect that you have been a victim to the tender passion."

George did not repel the insinuation, but seemed rather disposed to admit the soft impeachment.

"Well, Harry, I won't deny that for once in my life I was very near falling desperately in love. I had no chance of seeing her only when she came to our house about work, and then what trouble I had to put Ally and the old lady off the scent. It was something only to meet her as she passed through the hall. Yes, Clare, if I could have seen my way a little clearer, or if she had given me the least bit of encouragement, I believe I should have risked everything and tried my luck for life, but she never even looked at me, and there was something about her that kept one at a distance, for though she was so modest and quiet, she was as proud as a duchess in her way. I wish you could have seen her, Harry, such a splendid creature, beauty enough to make a room full of women mad with jealousy. I would give anything to be invited down to Woodlands, now she is there, but I had the ill luck to offend my cousin Fanny; but I think I see a way to repair the mischief. Dr. Marsh has a snug box in that neighbourhood. I will go down and pay my respects to his nephew, Cecil Lee, an old school chum of yours, Harry. You must remember him, for you often took him under your protecting wing; he was a quiet, delicate boy, with a face almost like a girl's, and some of the fellows used to call him Miss Cecil?"

"Ah, yes, I remember Lee," Harry replied; "it was quite a treat to me when I met him accidentally at the lakes about three years ago; since then I have lost sight of him."

"Well, then, Clare, come along with me, and we will take Woodlands by siege," exclaimed George, eagerly. "Ah, I did not think of it before. Lee has become a handsome, striking looking fellow, and he is getting himself much talked of as an artist; he may be a dangerous rival in the field. And now I recollect, it was his uncle who attended Miss Arnold through her fever."

"Arnold! did you say Arnold, George?" interrupted Harry, starting from his seat as if he had received an electric shock.

"Yes, of course, that's her name," replied George, bewildered at this unexpected outburst, and opening his eyes wide with astonishment, "what on earth is the matter, Clare?"

Harry had recovered himself by an effort, but his agitation was still too violent to allow him to speak calmly. "Nothing, Foster, only there is one of that name very dear to me, whom I have been vainly seeking for some time." He briefly explained his actual position, and enlightened his friend about his private affairs, as far as he judged it necessary.

George looked perplexedly on the carpet. There was a half-comic ruefulness in his face, as he said,

"Well, Clare, if it should turn out that this is your Miss Arnold, I shall say you are in luck, to have won such a creature; and I must give up Woodlands and all my castle-building in that quarter. Come, let us compare notes. What was she like? Was she tall and pale, a face like a picture, and brown hair and brown eyes? The sort of eyes that do the most mischief, and go straight to a man's heart before he is aware. I used to call her the evening star."

Harry winced at the freedom of this description, and acknowledged, with a little twinge of jealousy, that this portrait was strikingly like his own cherished original.

"It is, it must be the same, Foster. I little thought that I should owe so much to our chance meeting this afternoon. Tell me all you know of my dear Grace, how your cousin became acquainted with her, and what led to her being offered a home at Woodlands? I must know the full extent of my debt of gratitude to the generous friend who helped her in her time of need. It will be a painful story, Foster, but tell me all you can, without reserve; don't conceal anything from pity for my feelings. I have no wish to spare myself; but first answer me, was the late Mr. Arnold in great pecuniary distress during his last illness? Have you heard it said that poverty—want—had anything to do with his death?"

Harry had risen from his seat, and while he spoke, had been excitedly pacing the room. He now stopped suddenly before George's chair, repeating his last words in a voice that shook with suppressed feeling.

George Foster received this agitated torrent of questions with a startled, troubled look, and his smooth, unreflective face showed unusual signs of mental disturbance. There was genuine sympathy in his tone and manner as he blundered out his answer, crowding his words together with his characteristic want of respect for grammatical rules.

"Come, Clare, I can't bear to see you cut up like this, though at the same time I own that it's quite natural for you to feel strongly about all that concerns a—a—certain person. I'm sorry, for your sake, that I know next to nothing about what is making you so anxious; the reason is that I've been on the wrong side of our petticoat government ever since my unlucky affair with cousin Fanny, and I'm always kept in the dark about everything that goes on in the house. I do know that about the time her father died Miss Arnold left off working for my mother. I believe she was then in great need of help, and that my mother was to blame for it in a way that I don't like to think about; and I heard something whispered about your uncle, Harry, I don't know how true it might be."

"Tell me! tell me!" interrupted the listener with breathless eagerness, "what did you hear?"

"That Mr. Arnold owed him money, and when he lay ill your uncle went to their lodgings and tried to bully them, for some purpose of his own, which at such a time was a deuced cruel shame, and at last frightened her father into breaking a blood vessel."

"God forgive him!" burst from Harry's quivering lips in a low pained voice, that in its suppressed agony sounded like a groan. He resumed his agitated pacing of the floor.

Now he could understand all. Those few words brought a complete revelation to his startled mind; joining them with his own experience of his uncle's conduct since his return to England, he had the key to all that had troubled and perplexed him. By the aid of this new light he could read his actions, and the motives which had prompted them.

George arrested him by a friendly touch on his arm, his face full of the pleased importance of a new and happy idea.

"Tell you what, my dear fellow, there's nothing for it but to go down to Woodlands as soon as you can, and see her. That's my advice."

Harry roused himself by an effort.

"A very sensible suggestion, Foster. I will apply for a few days' holiday, and lose no time in acting upon it. I think I may venture to trust my geographical knowledge of the place as a sufficient guide, for I have been several times in the neighbourhood of Woodlands. If I remember right, it is within reach by an easy railway journey."

"Yes, you will do it in a couple of hours," remarked George.

"Will you go down with me, Foster?"

George coloured and busied himself with the box of cigars, as he answered with a little hesitating cough:

"Not this time, Harry, I should only be in the way. I must make up my mind to wait till I have made my peace with cousin Fan.

By the bye, Harry, you must observe her, she is worth studying; you would think so if you had seen her, as I have, with her great black eyes flashing fire at you, and her woman's tongue cutting like—"

Here poor George's powers of simile treacherously failed him. It was in vain, that he cudgelled his obdurate brains for an appropriate object of comparison, inspiration would not be invoked; so he was left, hopelesly floundering in the middle of his sentence. But to his relief Harry Clare was too much absorbed with his own thoughts, to notice his confusion or its cause.

By this time the rain had ceased, and the sky was clearing; it was not long before the two young men took advantage of the weather. They shook hands, George fervently wishing his friend luck, and Harry (in his turn) promising to drop a note from Woodlands, in which his movements should be faithfully chronicled; which proofs of confidence and consideration were intensely gratifying to George Foster, giving him more exalted ideas of his own personal importance, and flattering him into a state of very comfortable self-satisfaction.

## CHAPTER XI.

It was one of those intensely hot days, when we dream yearningly of running streams, and are conscious of irrepressible longings to be hidden from the universal, blinding glare, in some delicious green nook of coolness and shadow far away in the dusky twilight of some noble old forest, which the invading deluge of brick and mortar has not yet reached.

Harry Clare was toiling slowly and wearily down the road from Woodlands to the village. It was not fatigue that made him pause, lean heavily against a tree, and shading his eyes with his hand, look dejectedly back along the white line of road, that wound between luxuriant green hedges up to the park gate of Woodlands.

Disappointment, almost verging on despair, could be read in every line of his face. It was the reaction of powerfully stimulating excitement. The loss of a cherished hope, on which the spirit had sustained itself. He remembered how he traversed that same road, only a short time before, his heart full of Grace Arnold, and thrilling with joy at the thought of seeing her, and recalled his emotion at first sight of Woodlands, for he felt a sort of reverential love for the peaceful old grey house, which had given his unhappy suffering darling a home, when she most needed one. How longingly he had looked at the glistening windows, in fond, anxious search for that dearly loved face. But all his pleasant anticipation had been ruthlessly dispelled, by a few common-place words, from a very common-place person, viz., the Woodlands housekeeper (fat, good-humoured, and middle aged) whom he encountered at the hall door, who civilly informed him that the family had left Woodlands for the summer, considerately adding, that if he had come on important business, or if he had any letter to forward, he could see the steward, Mr. Dobson, who was the family's business agent, and always managed every-thing when they were away.

Harry Clare thanked her with his accustomed politeness, but turned hastily away, remarking that his business was of no present consequence; and it was not necessary to trouble Mr. Dobson.

He shrank almost with pain from the thought of placing himself in contact with a cool, dry, methodical man of business. He asked himself 'Should he write to Grace?' No; he had his own reasons for wishing to take her by surprise; for though he steadily refused to attach any significance to them, his uncle's poisoned words were still rankling in his mind. If any coldness towards him had crept into her heart; if time, absence, and the pressure of worldly cares had been fatal to the old love; the change would be at once revealed, in the first unguarded moment of an unexpected meeting, and would enable him, afterwards, to spare her much painful embarrassment. No; he would not write; letters were such cold, passionless things, such poor, feeble interpreters of the heart's language. He could not pour out on senseless paper the long pent-up tide of his feelings. He must see her. He retraced his way back to the village inn, repeating bitterly to himself, "Oh, Grace! when and where shall we meet?"

The chance-mention of Dr. Marsh's name, in the little inn parlour, recalled to his recollection his old school-friend, Cecil Lee; and also George Foster's parting advice to pay him a visit while he was in the neighbourhood. He seized eagerly upon this idea, surprised that it had not occurred to him before, and instantly prepared to act upon it. He remembered George had told him that Cecil Lee was intimate at Woodlands. Through him he would be sure to obtain, without further difficulty, all the information he sought. A very short time sufficed to negotiate with the burly good-humoured landlord for the hire of the best conveyance which he could place at the service of his guest. This was a gig, drawn by a sturdy brown pony; the landlord assuring Harry, with an air of proud satisfaction, that Bob was as cute as a Christian, and knew every yard of the roads round about; that he would wager him to find his way to the Doctor's of his own accord.

Harry could scarcely restrain his impatience till he found himself on the road, going at a smart pace. He urged Bob to a speed which must have been an unaccountable novelty in the experience of that respectable and highly-estimated animal; for whenever he showed a disposition to enter a protest against the new order of things, by relapsing into his usual jog-trot, a smart cut of the whip effectually roused his faculties, and made him prick up his ears in indignant astonishment.

By such means, Harry Clare accomplished the drive from the village to the Doctor's in about half the time that the pony usually appropriated for the journey.

Dr. Marsh's snug box, as George Foster called it, proved to be a charming little villa, most picturesquely situated, and commanding a beautiful landscape view, that would have endeared it to the heart of any artist. Fanny Templeton often saucily said that nature never intended it for a bachelor's abode—it looked far too pretty and comfortable.

As he approached the gate, Harry slackened the reins, and allowed the pony to go his own pace. As the gig wound slowly up the drive, past the trim box hedges, which inclosed it like a massive green wall, he had leisure to recover his self-possession, and prepare for the pleasant excitement of meeting his old school-friend.

But another disappointment awaited him.

The noise of wheels brought a middle-aged footman to the hall door, from whom he received the annoying intelligence that Mr. Cecil was gone from home, and not expected to return for some weeks, it might be longer, for Mr. Cecil's stay was always uncertain.

Harry bit his lip to conceal from the man how much this news discomposed him; he next asked to see Dr. Marsh.

Still the same irritating ill luck, the chances of the day were against him.

The Doctor was dining at the squire's, and would not return till late.

He was considering whether it would be best to leave his card, submit to the provoking delay of a day and night in the village, and return in the morning to see the doctor,—when his ear caught these words, spoken by a thin, reedy voice from the hall.

"A friend of Mr. Cecil's—Is it, Owen? perhaps he would like to alight, and rest a little."

Harry looked with some curiosity for the owner of the voice, and saw a tall, angular, young man, with light, perplexed eye-brows; weak, pale, blue eyes, defended by green spectacles; and short bristling red hair, that showed a perverse inclination to resist the discipline of comb and brush.

Harry rightly guessed this individual to be some humble satellite of the doctor's. The footman respectfully addressed him as Mr. Murray. He came forward with a diffident flush on his cheeks, and in the name of the absent doctor timidly proffered his invitation to Mr. Cecil's friend. It was at once accepted, with a ready, unhesitating eagerness that was highly gratifying to the simple-hearted youth in the green spectacles.

Harry Clare had certainly a motive in thus eagerly availing himself of the invitation to the doctor's house. He believed the hospitable Mr. Murray was domesticated as one of Dr. Marsh's family, and that he should be able to obtain from him all the information he sought. So he gladly resigned the reins to the smart dapper little groom, who just then made his appearance, and satisfied that Bob, the pony, would be well-cared for in such hands, followed his new friend into the doctor's library—a cool pleasant room, which was more suggestive of a natural history museum, to judge from the extensive collection of carefully-arranged zoological spcimens, in which the good doctor took no small pride. Mr. Murray courteously placed a chair for his visitor, and sat down himself in the seat which he seemed to have just quitted; for it was close to the reading table, and a huge folio was open before it. He made some abortive attempts at conversation, but got no further than a blundering comment upon the weather, and the surrounding scenery, to which he kept up a fidgetting accompaniment, by nervously playing with the leaves of his book.

The situation was becoming a little awkward. Harry was good-naturedly anxious to relieve the embarrassment of a nervous man, unaccustomed to society; and possessing the happy power of setting people at their ease, he soon succeeded in engaging the shy assistant in a conversation, in which he forgot his timidity, and carried along with his subject, talked naturally and well, for he was evidently a young man of education and extensive reading.

Harry learned that his name was Allan Murray; that he was an orphan—the son of a poor Scotch surgeon—a friend of the doctor's—who had been unfortunate in his profession, and had died early, in the midst of his struggles. The youth added, with grateful tears gathering in his eyes, that he would have been left destitute and friendless, but for the good doctor, who had defrayed the expense of his education, took him home as a companion for his nephew, Cecil, and was now preparing him for the medical profession, for which he had a strong inclination. Their talk then turned to Cecil Lee, and here a perfect freemasonry of thought and feeling seemed to exist between them. Chance had directed Harry's critical eye to a small picture in oils, which was inscribed "The dying sheep dog," and represented a noble animal, wounded by a random shot from some unlucky sportsman; with the film of mortal agony glazing his eyes, the poor mutely-eloquent brute was looking for his master, with piteous deprecating helplessness; and faithful to the last, seemed to be making a final despairing effort to bark out the accustomed summons to the scattered flock. It was a fine spirited sketch—not inferior to Landseer. The dog was a study into which the artist had thrown all his power.

The visitor lingered admiringly before the picture, but the enthusiastic Allan left him no time to make enquiries. "Ah!" he exclaimed, exultingly, "I was waiting to see if you would discover it. That is one of our Cecil's pictures; the doctor would not part with it at any price. But I must show you his studio, and his last picture; I may take the liberty in his absence; he will not be displeased as you are an old friend." If Harry Clare had any scruples about thus intruding into his friend's sanctuary without his knowledge, he had no opportunity of being influenced by them, for Allan had already taken a key from one of the table drawers, and unlocked and opened a side door which had, till now, escaped Harry's notice. The next moment he was hurried into the artist's painting room, or studio, as Allan Murray always called it.

"This room is under my own charge when Cecil is absent," he said with pardonable pride; "you are a worshipper of art, Mr. Clare; I read it in your look, here are two or three little things that will delight you; but this picture,—indicating one much larger than the rest, which was carefully covered,—I think you would have missed a treat, if you had gone away without seeing it; it is only waiting for the finishing touches, but I suspect that it will not make much further progress until Miss Templeton and her aunt return home. Pity you don't know the originals, for then you would be able to appreciate the striking correctness of the portraits."

"Is it intended for the Academy's exhibition?" asked Harry, whose interest was excited by the mention of Miss Templeton!

"No," replied Allan; "it is for the dining-room at Woodlands. I shall be sorry to part with it," continued Cecil's humble admirer; "I always feel so, whenever one of the pictures is removed; they seem like old friends, for which I have a sort of affection. I watch the beautiful creations growing into life, under Cecil's hand, until they seem to become a part of my existence. Look here, Mr. Clare!" and with far more triumphant pride than the artist himself would have exhibited, Allan Murray unveiled the picture; it was a sweet, simple sketch, deliciously rendered. A tranquil, happy household scene, given, as the newspaper critics would say, in the artist's best manner. The room gave a refreshing sense of coolness and shadow, pleasantly contrasted with the sunny garden view from the window. Nothing could be more beautiful than the grouping of the three figures round the little work-table, Fanny Templeton, with her favourite dog at her feet, most audaciously appropriating a portion of her dress for his cushion. How had the artist-lover lingered over this part of his work, as if he could never satisfy himself that he had done justice to the fascinations which had enslaved him! The arch, dark eyes seemed to be sparkling from the life-like canvass, and a bright, joyous smile was curving the ripe crimson lips. But all this beauty was lost upon ungrateful Harry Clare, whose entire capacity of gazing seemed to be concentrated upon the third member of the little sewing party. There was no mistaking that dear, well-remembered face. It was his own Grace. Here at least she was restored to him. Cecil's picture had given him back his lost love.

Allan watched him in wondering silence. He had noticed his start of surprise, when his glance first fell upon the picture. His wrapt attention, and absorbed manner of contemplation, might be interpreted into a flattering tribute to the artist's power; but it did not satisfy Allan's exacting admiration of Cecil. He wanted more demonstrative kind of praise, some enthusiastic outburst of admiration, and was more disappointed than he would have liked to acknowledge. It was a relief at that moment for Allan to be summoned away by the footman, Owen, who came to announce a visitor. The young man apologized for an interruption that would detain him for a short time, hastily explaining that a scientific friend of the doctor's, whom he had been expecting all the morning, had just called, to look over some new specimens, and consult some books of reference.

Harry willingly excused him, and was thankful when his new acquaintance withdrew into the library, carefully closing after him the door of communication, and leaving him in the solitude for which he had been longing ever since the sweet, sad face of Grace had flashed upon him from Cecil's picture, for associations had been awakened, and emotions roused, which he shrank from betraying in the presence of a stranger.

How was it, that after the first delighted thrill of surprise at the unexpected sight of Grace Arnold's portrait, the lover was conscious of a new strange feeling of pain? Whence arose the vague nameless jealousy that struck to his heart with a sudden pang, and left his face so darkly troubled? What was there to distress him, in this simple evidence of his friend's talent as a portrait painter? And why did he find himself repeating the careless and (till then) almost forgotten words of George

Foster, that Cecil Lee was "a handsome, striking looking fellow, and might be a dangerous rival in the field?" Cecil Lee wooing Grace in that old country house, where everything would favour him; and Grace herself learning to cherish the new love. How his spirit writhed under the self-inflicted torture of these thoughts. He tried to banish the jealous doubt, by repeating the resolution he had formed in the proud moment of unshaken confidence; that he would never distrust Grace Arnold upon any evidence short of actual proof; or believe that she was estranged from him, until they had once more met and parted, and their final sentence of separation had been spoken by her own lips.

There was nothing to convict Cecil Lee of tender feelings towards Grace Arnold. It was just as natural to suppose him in love with every fair lady who might sit to him for her portrait. Harry Clare was labouring under a most lover-like delusion, for he could not imagine that Grace Arnold could be any other than the chief centre of attraction to those round her, and the supreme light of the circle in which she moved.

He did not know how long he had stood before the picture, for he had been too much agitated to note the flight of time, when Allan Murray returned, congratulating himself that the somewhat tiresome old naturalist had made his visit shorter than he had anticipated.

They were soon chatting pleasantly together about Cecil, and the progress he was making in his art; and Allan, much to his own content, now found himself really doing the honours of the studio to Cecil's friend.

"By the bye, Mr. Murray," exclaimed Harry, as if struck by a sudden thought, "I have half decided to take a little tour round the country before I go back to London. Perhaps I may have the good fortune to come upon our wandering artist in some of his favourite haunts; if you will kindly furnish me with a few guiding hints, for my old friend is such a bird of passage that when once fairly on the wing it is almost impossible to—"

"But he is safe enough at present, Mr. Clare," interrupted Allan, laughing, "he is too well accompanied now to be in any danger of indulging his rambling propensities. If you have a fancy for sea bathing, and would like to run down to a quiet little nook on the coast not very far from here, I can give my word that you would be sure to find Mr. Cecil and his sketch book, besides getting the chance of being introduced to Miss—Miss Arnold—I think that is her name, the young lady whose portrait seemed to interest you so much just now. Do you know, I was beginning to fancy you might fall in love with her."

Jesting on such delicate subjects was very unusual with the shy, timid Allan. As he concluded the last sentence he blushed to the roots of his hair at the thought of his own boldness, and the impression it might make upon the dignified-looking stranger. But to his relief his little stroke of raillery did not seem even to have been noticed; there was not the slightest change in Mr. Clare's look or manner, as he said:

"Am I to understand that Mr. Cecil has joined the Woodlands party in their search for pleasure and health? I suppose the excursion is intended to unite both objects?"

"Yes," replied Allan, again blushing, "he is the ladies' protector and cavalier, but I think he will not mind dividing the honour with you. The doctor himself will be going down towards the end of the week, for he is anxious about Miss Templeton's friend; she is in ill health, rather a serious case; but he depends much on the effect of sea air and change of scene."

Harry turned pale, and smothered a cry of pain that was nearly wrung from him by this revelation.

Allan Murray was just then busy re-covering the pictures, and did not observe his agitation. Before they went back to the library he had time to regain his self-possession, and decide upon his plans. Once he half resolved to seek the sympathy and advice of the affectionate, warm-hearted Allan—reveal to him the fact of the long engagement existing between himself and Grace Arnold; and while explaining his own position, contrive to sound his knowledge of Cecil's feelings, for the young man's own words had tended to confirm his suspicion that the Woodlands party possessed something more than ordinary attraction for the young artist. But he instinctively shrank from this confidence, and preferred to accept even the torturing uncertainties of a lover's suspense, with all its feverish alternations, between jealous, unjust doubt, and blind, unlimited trust.

"I hope you will decide, Mr. Clare, to go down and give Cecil a pleasant surprise," said Allan, taking a slip of paper, and drawing the inkstand towards him.

"Yes, I will go. I would not lose the opportunity for all I have in the world," replied Harry, turning round with a sort of suppressed eagerness in his manner. "Ah, what is this?—the address? Thanks, Mr. Murray. I must acknowledge myself indebted to your practical good sense, for it is more than probable that I should have forgotten to ask for it." He glanced over the written card which Allan handed to him, and placed it carefully in his pocket book, adding, "I think I know this place. It is a pretty, primitive village on the West Coast. I hope I shall be able to get down this evening."

As he spoke he took out his Bradshaw, and was soon engaged in profound study of that traveller's oracle, for he was feverishly impatient to be on his way.

"Ah, this will just suit me," he exclaimed eagerly, taking out his watch; "fortune smiles for once; there is a train, and I shall just be able to get back to the village in time."

"Going so soon?" said Allan, with a little regret in his voice, for he had really begun to like his new acquaintance, and felt his society to be an agreeable diversity to the monotony of his quiet, uneventful life. "Then you will not wait to see the doctor?"

"No," replied Harry. "I must sacrifice that pleasure, as business only allows me a few days' absence, I am compelled to make the most of my time."

The young men shook hands cordially and parted, mutually pleased with each other.

Allan Murray stood at the library window until the gig was out of sight. Then, with a little, regretful sigh, he went meekly back to his reading of the large folio, and took up the broken thread of his solitary studies, now and then diverting his mind with the unselfish pleasure of picturing the gay sea-side meeting between two old friends, for in Cecil Lee's reminiscences of school life, Allan had often heard the young artist sound the praise of Harry Clare.

# CHAPTER XII.

A WHITE cottage, charmingly hidden behind rugged, wave-washed cliffs. It stood in that quiet sheltered sea-nook, like a pearl in a green casket. A dainty bird-nest of a dwelling, that looked as if the fairies had once designed it for their home, and had dropt it there, in some of their moonlight revels. There was a sunny strip of green lawn, enclosed by a low white wall, and a pretty rustic gate, whilst the glistening windows were draped with climbing wild roses. Fanny Templeton was almost wild with delight when she first went down, voted it the loveliest spot in the world, and declared that she should never want to leave Cliff Cottage.

It was no marvel that Cecil Lee should be always there. Nominally, he occupied rooms at an hotel at the neighbouring watering place. But knowing what we do of his feelings towards the fair heiress of Woodlands, it was only natural that he should find Cliff Cottage more attractive than the busy haunts where the crowd of pleasure-seekers loved to congregate. He pronounced it the finest sea-view. No other place seemed to inspire his pencil, though the neighbourhood was rich in material that an artist is supposed to covet. It had a curious old church, with some historical interest to distinguish it, and a ruined abbey, which he did not even notice till Fanny Templeton drew his attention to it. But he was never tired of sketching Cliff Cottage and its surroundings. He had taken that diminutive white house from every point of view. Quite natural under the circumstances, for the artist was in love, and Cliff Cottage was then the shrine of his divinity.

The ladies had been nearly a fortnight domesticated in their new home; when, one bright morning, Fanny broke gaily into the little sunny parlour, where Grace was enjoying a quiet chat with Aunt Margaret, who was engaged in her favourite occupation, knitting winter stockings for her poor old pensioners at Woodlands.

"What a charming morning for our sail," exclaimed Fanny, with a pretty affectation of childish joy, "and what a delightful opportunity it will be for Mr. Cecil to display his seamanship as commander of the Ocean Pearl. We ought to consider ourselves highly favoured. Don't you think so, most grave and reverend ladies?" and Fanny, laughingly, wound her arm round her aunt's neck, to the serious derangement of her neat cap border.

"My dear," replied the old lady, in a tone of affected reproof, "what would your aunt

Foster say to this unceremonious way of invading a quiet room."

"My aunt Foster," repeated Fanny; and she proceeded to mimic the tone and manner of the London lady, striking out her individual traits with graphic fidelity. "Oh! she would say, of course, that I was dreadfully abrupt and unladylike, that I had no proper pride, and a great deal more in the same strain, and my cousin Alice would freeze a little more, and look at me in her cold speculating way, as if I was a new species of animal, whom she was doubtful how to treat.

At that moment a glance through the window arrested her in the full tide of her humour. She turned away laughing and blushing, saying hastily: "Cecil is at the gate, as usual, punctual to the minute, and we have not yet begun to dress. Come, Grace, we must make our escape, for we have really not a moment to lose, if we intend to have our sail this morning."

And Fanny playfully seized her friend's arm, by way of adding force to her argument.

A few moments after, Cecil Lee entered the parlour, in high spirits at the beauty of the weather, and the prospect of pleasure which the day seemed to promise. But he found Aunt Margaret alone, a circumstance that caused him some secret disappointment. His patience was not long tried, for Fanny and Grace soon returned dressed for the morning's excursion, and followed by Morris, with a pile of cloaks and shawls over her arm.

Aunt Margaret had put aside her knitting, and was nervously interrogating the eagerly expectant lover.

"I confess that I am not quite easy about this sailing, Cecil, you think there is no positive danger; forgive a timid old woman's fears, for you know I am committing a precious trust into your hands."

"I am not likely to forget it, dear madam,

nor anything that involves the safety of life far dearer to me than my own."

There was a trembling in his voice, as he said those simple words.

Fanny gaily interposed: "My dear aunt, I am afraid that you will overwhelm our unfortunate cavalier with such a sense of his serious responsibilities, that he will be frightened into resigning his office." Blushing and smiling, she turned to Cecil, as she spoke; and their eyes met in one single thrilling glance, that was more eloquent than words, in which for one brief moment, Cecil lived again the rapture of a memorable twilight walk among the trees at Woodlands, not very long ago, with a dark brilliant face beside him, when he tried to read his future in its shifting lights and shadows; and staked all his hopes of happiness on one little word from those ripe red lips.

Fanny lingered behind the rest to kneel on her aunt's footstool, and whisper fondly:—

"Tell me, dear Aunt Maggie, will you feel dull and lonely while we are away?"

"No, darling, I shall take my walk when Morris comes back. She will go with you to the boat, and see you all comfortably seated, then she will return and give me a faithful report about you. But, dear child, what a pity that you are all going before lunch. How will ycu arrange?"

"Oh, Cecil will manage, aunt. He is an excellent caterer for such occasions; and seems to have a natural talent for providing. He likes everything to be left to him. But mind, we shall take care not to miss your nice hot dinner. It will be our lawful reward after the excitement of the day. Take care of yourself, aunty; and now, kiss me quick, and good morning, see, they are coming back to look for me."

As Fanny went out she carried with her a vivid impression of her Aunt's quiet figure in the sunny parlour, and the loving parting glance of her mild blue eyes. She could not tell why, but a shadow clouded her bright face as she lost sight of the white cottage; and for a moment, the excursion on the water was associated in her mind with vague, undefined feelings of uneasiness and regret. But Cecil had planned it solely for their pleasure, and dear Grace would be sure to enjoy the bracing air. No, she would not selfishly disappoint them, for the sake of her own foolish, unaccountable caprice.

## CHAPTER XIII.

At last it was over. The pleasant little bustle of the embarkation, from which Cecil contrived to extract some rare moments of lover's bliss, made up of such apparently inconsiderable items as the arrangement of a cushion, the pressure of a small gloved hand upon his arm, and the guiding of a dainty little foot to the boat's side, with the delicious sense of being depended upon, and looked up to for protection and support by the one best loved in the world.

He rendered the same kind offices to Grace, and surrounded her with the same solicitous care, but the gentle girl did not give him half so much trouble as the wilful, exacting, fascinating sprite, whom he had made the mistress of his fate. Grace Arnold was endeared to him by the fact that she was Fanny's friend. He admired her pure spiritual loveliness with the same kind of admiration that he would have given to a picture, or any other beautiful work of art. But her misfortunes, and her gentle, graceful manners, gave her other powerful claims upon his regard, which the refined and generous Cecil was not slow to recognise.

Morris stood tenaciously fixed in her post of observation, straining her eyes after the party in the boat, until they ached with the effort. She was just able to discern the little white handkerchief, which her beloved young mistress was gaily waving as a parting signal to dear, foolish old nurse. She might have been reassured by the rich, mellow, manly voice which suddenly broke upon the fresh morning air—

"A life on the ocean wave,
A life on the rolling deep—"

Floated full and clear over the water; but the old servant was perversely prejudiced. She turned away, murmuring to herself:—

"That's just like Mr. Cecil, he believes all the song says, as if any sensible people would ever think of spending their lives on the water. Well, I hope no ill will come of all this pleasure sailing. After all, Mr. Cecil is a very fine young man, and I don't know anyone that I should better like to see making up to my young lady."

The old nurse looked meditatively at the water, but she seemed then to be occupied with some picture in her own mind, to the exclusion of external objects. She came out of her reverie with a stifled sigh—

"Well, well, it's the law of nature, and we must submit. We can't keep our nurselings always for our own. They will grow up and be fallen in love with, and married before our eyes. I am selfish to be fretting because my

M

darling is a woman grown, and has found some-one to love her as well as her aunt and her silly old nurse."

And again straining her eyes to catch a last glimpse of the boat, which had become a mere speck upon the water, faithful, simple-hearted Morris turned away from the beach, and took her way slowly and thoughtfully back to Cliff Cottage.

The Ocean Pearl was an object of absorbing interest to another beside the old servant, and the unconscious little group of pleasure seekers were watched by other eyes with a distrustful scrutiny, which had something painfully intense in it.

If the attention of Morris had not been otherwise engrossed she would have noticed perhaps with some feminine curiosity, a light-oared boat, which seemed to be idly coquetting with the water, for it lay like a feather on the glistening waves, gracefully rising and falling with the swell of the advancing tide. It contained three figures, one a tall, gentlemanly young man, who had been for some time intently watching the movements of the boating party through a pocket telescope.

His companions were an old fisherman, whose brown weather-beaten face, notched and wrinkled by time, bore evidence of a life early inured to privation and hardship; and his nephew, a wiry, active lad of sixteen, who was amusing himself by watching the abstracted moody stranger who had powerfully excited his organ of wonder, and listening with a sort of lazy attention to the monosyllabic remarks that were from time to time exchanged between the gentleman and his uncle. He watched his opportunity, when under pretence of doing something to one of the oars he could stoop down and whisper to the old man:

"I say, Uncle Jim, it's time to put off now, if the gen'lman's ever going to have his sail, seems to me he'll never be tired of spying that bit of canvass out yonder."

"Hold hard, Dan, and don't be meddling with your betters," responded his relative, in a sharp, admonitory whisper. "The gen'man's hired the boat, and may please hissel' for the rest you've got to say nothin' about it, so be quiet, youngster, before your prying brings you into trouble."

The lad good-humouredly shrugged his shoulders, puffed out his cheeks, and curving one of his hard brown fingers into the form of a whistle, applied it slyly to his mouth with a broad grin of intelligence that highly provoked his uncle.

At that moment the gentleman accidentally dropped his telescope into the bottom of the boat. It was officiously picked up by Dan, and restored to its owner with much awkward civility, for he was conscious that Uncle Jim's sharp grey eyes were watching him closely.

The stranger thanked him kindly, then pulled his hat down over his brow, and gave a hasty order for the boat to be rowed off.

A few minutes more and they were skimming smoothly and swiftly over the water, the steady splash of their oars mingling pleasantly with the soft gurgling ripple of the waves breaking against the boat's side. They had taken the same course as the Ocean Pearl, whether by accident or design did not appear, but it was certain that the little boat with its well skilled rowers was rapidly gaining on the track of its more ambitious rival, for the gay pleasure boat and its passengers were now distinctly visible.

"Tidy craft that, sir," remarked old Jim, the fisherman, respectfully pointing it out to the stranger; "she's about as neat rigged and pretty a little thing for show as one could find, but she ain't fit for all weathers."

"Why, yon's the ladies from Cliff Cottage, and the young gen'lman as is going to marry one of 'em," struck in young Dan, turning up his shrewd face in affected simplicity, but at the same time slyly watching the gentleman's face, for he had some precocious thoughts of his own about that 'ere bit of canvass; he afterwards told his uncle that he was dead sure it hadn't been spied at so long through that telescope for noth'n.

"Why, Dan, how come you to know 'em?" asked the old fisherman, secretly proud of the lad's quickness.

The susceptible Dan coloured to the tips of his ears as he acknowledged the source of his information.

"Oh, Sally told me; she knows, for she's always helping the servants up at the Cottage. They're both uncommon nice ladies, and the little 'un has heaps of money, Sally says. But the one that's been ill I like best, cause she look so like a pictur."

The strange gentleman was listening with a marked appearance of interest. The grave lines in his face had softened, and his thoughtful mouth had relaxed into a smile. Young Dan was honoured with more particular notice than had yet fallen to his share.

He was growing confused under the observation which he had drawn upon himself, when, much to his relief, an exclamation from his uncle at once diverted the gentleman's attention. It referred to the Ocean Pearl, which the old fisherman had been silently watching for some minutes. The two boats were now so near that they almost caught the flutter of the ladies' dresses, and could clearly distinguish the murmur of low voices, pleasantly mingled with bursts of gay laughter.

"They 'ill be going too far out," he muttered, almost angrily, with a vehement motion of the oars. "If I had the care of them two bonny bairns, I should look a long way ahead and keep a sharp eye to windward afore I ventur'd. As for that lubberly blockhead they've got at the helm, I should like to overhaul him!"

"Surely you do not apprehend danger," remarked the stranger, anxiously.

The old fisherman answered somewhat evasively:—

"I dunno say exactly as I do, only if I was

that young gen'lman, I shouldn't care to have them two young creatures aboard yon cockle shell in a squall, pretty and neat rigged as she is."

"But on such a morning as this there can be no fear," returned the gentleman, trying to smile, and drawing a deep breath, as if to relieve himself from some oppressive feeling.

The old man puckered up the corners of his mouth, and set his head back with a calm consciousness of superior knowledge, mingled with a slight dash of pity for the landsman's ignorance, and an air that plainly said, "Whatever difference there may be between us two ashore, here I'm at home, and able to teach you something."

He said, quietly:—

"Don't be too sure of that, sir—the wind's been rising this half hour, and there's a little cloud over there, no bigger than our Dan's cap, that I don't half like. Lor bless you, sir, the sea's as changeable, and little to be trusted, as—" he paused for a fitting object of comparison, and taking off his cap, ran his fingers through his short bush of grey hair, by way of stimulating his brains, then added, with a humourous twinkle in his eyes:—"As little to be trusted as a woman."

The stranger paid little heed to these last words, for he was anxiously examining the sky, which had become suddenly overcast. The wind was rising with a sullen moaning sound, and a dull lurid light seemed to be cast on the water.

The uneasy motion of the boat, which now put to the test all the skill and strength of the rowers, fully justified the forebodings of the old fisherman.

"Knew we should have it before long, sir; but it 'ill be on us sooner than I looked for. I doubt we shall have a bit of rocking fore we can put ashore—we're used to it—but you—"

He was abruptly interrupted by the stranger, who caught him excitedly by the arm, and pointing to the gay looking pleasure boat in advance of them, exclaimed, breathlessly:—

"Surely, surely, they will not be so mad as to venture any further out with those ladies!"

The old boatman stole a sly questioning side-glance at him, as he answered:

"Canna tell, sir, but if they do it'll strain her canvas a bit, and make her show what stuff she's made of."

"I have all the morning had my doubts about that gay looking painted thing," the gentleman broke in hastily. "See how she struggles, the gale is getting fiercer every moment. Ah, that last gust has told upon her, she has lost one of her sails. Oh, Grace, Grace! so near, and yet so far from me, it will be dreadful to lose you thus." And in a paroxysm of excited feeling, he suddenly started from his seat, and, regardless of any personal peril, stood as if meditating some blind act of reckless daring.

The old boatman caught his arm, in genuine alarm and astonishment; a quick glance of intelligence was exchanged between him and his nephew, which might have been thus interpreted:

"Poor gentleman! must be a little bit touched in the head part; fancies he knows somebody out yonder. Thought he was queerish at first; and doubt we shall have a job with him afore we puts ashore."

* * * *

"Grace, Grace, what is the matter? You look pale and faint, lean on me, dear. Why you are positively trembling; this is foolish. Courage, courage! Cecil says we have nothing to fear;" and as she tenderly stooped over the agitated girl, softly caressing the slight pale hand, and doing her best to reassure her—Fanny Templeton turned and cast one bright expressive glance at Cecil Lee, who was standing near, conversing with one of the sailors. It was scarcely a moment before the eloquent black eyes were hastily lowered, but not before the lover had caught their glance, and gathered to his heart the intoxicating flattery of the whisper—"Cecil says we have nothing to fear;" it was so full of delicious meaning, and implied such sweet womanly trust and dependence on him. When he joined them he did his best to confirm the cheering assurance which Fanny had just given to her friend, though he had a certain uneasy sense of responsibility, and a cruel weight of secret anxieties, which he was careful to conceal from his fair companions.

"What makes me most uncomfortable," said Fanny, in a low voice, to Cecil, in reply to some tender inquiry, "is that I fear the after effect of this excitement upon our invalid, and then, dear Aunt Maggie, I am afraid that foolish old Morris will infect her with all sorts of exaggerated alarms. If it were not for these considerations, Cecil, I am vain enough to think that my courage would be quite equal to the occasion; and perhaps I might rather enjoy the situation."

As she spoke, a huge angry crested wave

broke over the boat, scattering a shower of white spray at her feet. It was at that moment one of the sails was torn away by an unusually fierce gust of wind, and the frail boat, with its precious freight of thrilling, loving, human hearts, was left blindly struggling with the remorseless fury of the storm.

Looking at the wild threatening storm clouds, and the angry foaming waves, madly leaping and lashing each other in their tempestuous wrath, it was difficult to realise the fair picture of a few hours before, and believe that these were the same waters which had slept so tranquilly in the sunshine, and filled the ear with such soft dreamy murmurs.

Grace shivered and crept nearer to Fanny, every delicate fibre of her sensitive frame thrilling and trembling with nervous agitation. Fanny's bearing was characteristic; instinctively drawing the folds of the heavy shawl closer round Grace, and tightening her arm round the slight waist, she stood with her small head thrown back, her lips compressed into a slender crimson line, her fine, dark eyes dilating, and her calm, pale face looking resolutely out upon the surging waves.

Cecil Lee was near them, trying to do a man's work with a man's spirit; resolved to save the lives of Fanny Templeton and her friend or lose his own in the effort.

It was at that moment that they distinctly caught the sound of oars rising above the noise of the waves, and for the first time noticed the gallant little fishing boat.

"Another party of unfortunate pleasure seekers, like ourselves, beguiled by the treacherous beauty of the weather, this morning," said Cecil. "I wonder if—"

But here his words were abruptly cut short by a low, startled cry from Grace Arnold, who sprang from Fanny's restraining arm, pointing to the other boat, with breathlessly extended hand, and excitedly exclaiming:

"Harry Clare! Yes, I am sure, it is he."

This dear name had scarcely broke from her pale, quivering lips, and she was still trembling with agitation, when a sudden heaving of the boat deprived her of her insecure footing. It was but the work of an instant, while the unconscious girl was leaning forward, unaware of her danger. The next moment Fanny Templeton, who had made a convulsive effort to save her friend, was standing, white and bewildered, with the corner of a scarf which the poor girl had worn, clasped tightly in her hand. Grace had fallen overboard, and the heiress of Woodlands would have shared the same fate, if the strong arm of Cecil Lee had not interposed in time to restrain her first rash impulse of generosity.

"Save her! Oh, save her!" she cried in despairing agony, as the brown head disappeared from her sight.

But before the echo of her voice had died away, before her words had time to influence any one around her, there was a daring plunge into the water, and a bold, fearless swimmer was gallantly breasting the waves in the direction where a heap of light female drapery might be seen at intervals floating on the water.

It was Harry Clare, whom Grace had recognised, the stranger gentleman from the fishing boat, who had jealously claimed the privilege of being the first to risk his life for the being so long and faithfully loved.

There was a merciful lull in the storm as he came on, followed by straining eyes, watching him in intense breathless expectation. Again and again they saw him on the point of grasping the form which he was making such superhuman efforts to reach; and as often they saw them separated by the white-crested waves, and the swimmer baffled and beaten back. Still the brave heart failed not. At last, when the breathless uncertainty of the struggle was becoming torture to those who watched, and just when the dear head had risen for the last time, a long, loud, exulting cheer rose from the two boats, for the gallant swimmer was bearing a slight figure in his arms. It was thus that Grace Arnold and Harry Clare met after their long separation.

In the effort to reach the boat, they might have shared a watery grave together, but for the timely help of young Daniel, the fisherman's nephew, for the brave swimmer, encumbered by the weight of the fainting girl, was becoming exhausted.

It was owing to the kindly care of the rough but humane old boatman, and the providential chance of his having brought with him a flask of brandy, that Grace was restored to life and consciousness.

The storm had now nearly spent its fury.

The boats were welcomed with a cheer, by a small excited crowd of people, consisting chiefly of natives of the village, mingled with a few strangers from the neighbouring bathing place, who had collected on the beach, watching their movements with breathless interest, and anxiety.

Grace felt like one in a dream. She saw

and heard all that passed around her; submitted to be tended and cared for, like a child, with a kind of passive unquestioning gentleness. She was blissfully conscious of having her hand clasped in some one's, and hearing her name murmured by a well-known voice, in low tender tones that woke the slumbering echoes of happy memories. But a troubled indefinable shadow seemed to lie between the past and present. Her senses seemed under the influence of a spell. She was conscious of being kissed, and wept over, by Fanny Templeton; and witnessed the meeting and friendly recognition between Cecil Lee and Harry Clare.

At another time, the discovery that the young men had been school friends, would have pleased and interested her, but now her mind was too much enfeebled to make any independent effort of thought. At present, she could only passively receive impressions.

She resigned herself to a quiet negative sort of happiness, in the sense of being softly shawled and cushioned, and borne along in the easy luxurious motion of a carriage. The last she remembered of that eventful morning, was the pleasant little surprise of being helped out at the cottage gate, by good, blustering Dr. Marsh himself, who had just arrived at a most opportune moment, in time to sooth away many of Aunt Margaret's fears; take charge of his gentle patient, and administer an affectedly severe reprimand to his nephew, Cecil, as the chief projector of the excursion, which had nearly ended so mournfully.

## CHAPTER XIV.

It was a week before the Doctor would allow Grace to leave her room. A weary, anxious week to Harry Clare, who still lingered in the vicinity of Cliff Cottage, daily persecuting Aunt Margaret and Fanny with innumerable inquiries about the invalid. But he was always treated with the most friendly forbearance, for he had unconsciously won his way to the hearts of both ladies. Fanny became one of his warmest advocates, and with characteristic enthusiasm determined that the lovers should meet on the first day that Grace left her sick room.

Much to the surprise and regret of Cecil Lee, he found that Harry Clare did not respond to his friendly advances, in the old cordial spirit. There was a strange coldness between them, a secret feeling of restraint, which he was at a loss to explain. In vain he reviewed the past, trying to discover some forgotten circumstance, in which he might unwittingly have given some offence, which had rankled in his friend's memory. On his side, Harry was tortured by jealous doubt and distrust, feelings so alien to his generous, candid nature. He was at a loss how to reconcile the artist's very marked attentions to Miss Templeton with his own preconceived conviction that he was in love with Grace Arnold; a conviction which he had based on no more reasonable foundation, than the lover-like fancy, that Grace must be always the principal object of attraction and pursuit, to any unmarried member of his own sex, with whom she might chance to be thrown into familiar communication.

If Harry Clare had acted towards Cecil with his usual frankness and generosity, he would have learned the truth, and the demon of jealousy would have been at once exorcised. It cannot be denied, that there was unkindness and injustice in his treatment of his old school friend. It was one of those jarring inconsistencies often found in the most perfect characters, an alloy of human weakness and infirmity, mingled with the pure, tried gold, of a noble nature.

Fanny was true to the promise which she had given Harry Clare.

On the first afternoon that Grace made her appearance in the cheerful little parlour, Fanny commenced operations by demurely informing her that it was very likely Mr. Clare would call, as he was compelled to return to town in a day or two, adding, that, for that afternoon, the task of entertaining him would devolve entirely upon herself, as she and Aunt Maggie would be particularly engaged. She then drew the little stand, with its freshly filled vase of flowers, up to the sofa where Grace sat, provided her with the new books which Cecil had sent up the evening before, and with a smiling, satisfied glance round the room, prepared to make a retr

Grace begged her to stay; but Miss Templeton obstinately refused, enforcing her decision by some whispered words which must have referred to the expected visitor, for Grace listened with drooping eye-lids, and a flood of crimson drifting into her pale face.

"Be wise in time, dear Grace, listen to the promptings of your own woman's heart, and don't let any foolish pride come between you, for I know you love each other. And, Grace, be sure you produce the letter you received from his uncle at Woodlands. Do not spare that vindictive old man; he had no pity for you, and your father, and he has deceived his nephew, it is fit that his own treachery should convict him."

Everything went on in harmony with

Fanny's wishes. As the weather was warm and bright, she had no difficulty in transplanting gentle Aunt Margaret, and her knitting, to the sheltered rustic seat in the garden, where she also transferred herself, with her sketch book and pencils, by way of keeping the dear old lady company, and securing the little parlour against unseasonable intrusion.

Cecil Lee had not paid his accustomed visit to the Cottage that day—being unavoidably detained at his hotel, where he was engaged to dine with a party of artist friends, newly arrived from town. Fanny tried to persuade herself that his absence just then was a very desirable relief. But she was unusually silent and subdued that afternoon, unusually disposed to think instead of talk—to sit with her pencil idly suspended in her hand, dreaming, and listening to the plaintive sea murmurs.

o o o o

At last, thanks to Fanny's management,

Harry Clare found himself alone with Grace. He saw her fair cheek flush as she rose from the sofa on his entrance, felt her dear hand tremble in his clasp, and watched her soft eyes fill with tears as she alluded to her accident, and spoke of the peril he had braved for her sake.

Those few touching words sunk into his heart, her thanks were very precious to him. Still the jealous, exacting spirit of the lover was not satisfied. He tormented himself with the thought that her emotion might only have arisen from the circumstances under which they had met; that it might be nothing more than the natural tribute of gratitude to the preserver of her life. He missed, or fancied he missed, something in the touch of her hand, the tone of her voice, something that was wanting to bring back the charm of the old time, and restore her to him as the Grace of the past.

After the first few minutes there was an embarrassing silence, both were conscious of a nameless feeling of restraint. He could not tell whether the cause existed in himself or Grace, but he felt that this was not the perfect re-union of which he had so fondly dreamed.

Yet never, in all the past days of happiness and prosperous fortune, before the struggle with the world had come, when the fresh, early bloom was on her young beauty, and the shadows of care and sorrow had not fallen on her brow, never, even in those bright days, had she seemed to him more lovely and loveable than now, when her frail, wasted figure, and pale, spiritual face told of the ordeal of sickness and suffering through which she had passed.

It was not her beauty alone that had won him. He could repeat now what he had told his uncle; that he loved Grace Arnold for something more precious and enduring.

He was the first to break the awkward silence.

"Ours was a strange meeting, Grace," he said with much feeling. "Thank God, that

I was permitted to save you in that hour of peril! But you overrate my service. The man is a selfish coward who would not do as much to save a fellow-creature's life. I can claim no merit to myself, for the act secured its own reward. My heart had recognised you, Grace; I knew that my life would be utterly useless and hopeless, if I lost the treasure I was trying to save."

Her cheeks flushed into brighter colour, and her beautiful brown eyes fell beneath his gaze. She held out her hand and tried to smile, but her voice trembled as she murmured slowly, and softly:

"Then it was all false. You are come back unchanged, and the past is something more than a memory."

He fervently kissed the little white hand, his jealous doubts and fears melting into air. Those few words satisfied the restless craving of his heart. He felt that Grace was worthy of a life's love and trust, that she was all he had believed her, simple, pure hearted, and true.

But even that moment of happiness had an alloy of pain. "My uncle's influence," he said mentally; "he has assailed my happiness in a way I could not suspect, for he has tried to rob me of her love and confidence." "Grace, you will confide in me," (he spoke with anxious earnestness). "I know that I have been misrepresented to you, and that chance circumstances may have helped to give some colour of truth to the falsehood. You will tell me all, and let me justify myself."

With a trembling hand Grace drew out her pocket book, and took from it the letter which she received at Woodlands from old Matthew Clare, and which Fanny Templeton had urged her to show Harry.

She silently placed it in his hand, but there was no feeling of resentful triumph against the old man, only a heartfelt regret that she could not spare Harry the pain of discovering his uncle's utter unworthiness of affection and respect.

"Thanks for this confidence, Grace," he whispered, as he opened the letter.

One rapid glance possessed him of its contents; his eyes caught an angry light, and his face flushed painfully; the first indignant impulse was to crush the paper in his hand, but he constrained himself and carefully re-read it.

Grace timidly touched his hand. It was a slight action, but it moved him much, and chased many troubled thoughts, for it assured him of her sympathy and participation in all that pained him.

"Dear one!" (he spoke hurriedly, as if not quite sure of his power of self-control); "this was a cruel shaft, and it was cruelly aimed! but it fell pointless, and disarmed of power to wound, for you trusted me, Grace."

Her clear frank look met his without shrinking, and her low voice was steady and unfaltering as she replied:

"Yes, Harry, I did trust you here, for my heart revolted against such a view of your character as that letter gave me. I felt that I could not so far have mistaken you, that whatever change time and absence might have affected in your feelings towards me, it was not in your nature to seek to insult and humiliate. The exaggeration of the falsehood caused its own detection. If your uncle had confined himself to the announcement of your engagement and intended marriage, he might have been believed. But that you should desire to renew our former acquaintance for the sake of gratifying your vanity at my expense, that was an excess of unmanly cruelty and meanness to which I knew you would never stoop."

She half turned away her face to hide her heightened colour and the tears that were filling her eyes.

His agitation was even greater than her own, as he said:—

"I never dreamed of this, my poor Grace! how severely your faith and patience have been tried. Why did you not write and tell me all? It might have spared us both much suffering; and I had a right, above all others to share your troubles. Grace dearest, since we parted, you have lived through many sad, dreary hours, when there seemed to be no light behind the clouds, when your trust in me was shaken, and the future looked all dark and hopeless. There is the shadow of that sorrowful time in your eyes now—tell me, Grace, have I not guessed the truth?"

"Yes," she answered, low and tremulously, with a rush of painful thoughts and memories —then added, with a touching tone of appeal in her voice:—

"It was agony to doubt you, Harry, but I could not help it sometimes. It was that cruel silence. If you had only written from

India as you promised (even my poor father fretted at the disappointment), your letters would have been such comfort in those blank weary days; something to live upon."

She had been suffered to go on, because he had no power to interrupt her. He listened with a sharp sense of pain, followed by a sick aintness. His sudden paleness frightened Grace.

He spoke in a slow, startled tone, as if the words cost him an effort.

"What does this mean, Grace? There must be some painful mystery;—do you say that you never received any letters from India?"

"Not one!" was her low distinct answer.

"And I wrote to you by every mail."

This was gasped out, rather than spoken, with a painful spasmodic working of the muscles of the mouth. For a moment he averted his face, as if he could not bear to read in the dear brown eyes that were watching him so wistfully, the confirmation of his own conviction of his uncle's treachery, and cruel abuse of confidence.

When he again turned to Grace there was a burning flush on his cheeks, and the dark, earnest eyes had a tearful glitter in them, but no drops fell. His voice had gathered something of sternness, but it broke down in a burst of feeling, as he said:—

"Oh, Grace, I cannot tell you how deeply I feel this. I might have spared you much suffering, darling, if I had made more prudent arrangements, if I had trusted less. But how could I suspect such treason in my father's brother? how could I dream that he would thus dishonour the family name which it has always seemed one of his ruling passions to lift up to distinction? I know how ruthlessly he would have punished such an act in one of his clerks or dependents. Grace, I would endure much to have this undone; for however harsh and unjust his anger and mistaken ambition may make him deal with me, it would take away all the bitterness to know, at least, that he had not sunk below respect."

There was an agitated earnestness in his look and tone, that gave a passionate force to his words, and told how painfully sensitive he was on the subject of his uncle's dishonourable breach of confidence. Grace knew that he felt strongly. Her sympathy could divine the nature and depth of the wound. It was inexpressively soothing to him, at that moment, to feel the unsolicited touch of her cool, soft hand, and have his painful thoughts broken in upon by her low, gentle whisper.

"We must pity and forgive, Harry; your uncle has injured himself most of all. Think of his lonely old age."

"You are right, dearest," replied Harry, much moved. "He has closed his heart, by his own will isolated himself from affection and sympathy, and now, nothing remains but disappointment—the bitter fruit of wasted energies, and a life blindly sacrificed to selfish mistaken aims. But, dear Grace, my uncle does not deserve that you should plead for him. I know he has been hard and cruel to you and yours."

Her eyelids drooped, and her lip trembled, for those words recalled the closing scene of her father's sufferings, and brought vividly back the anguish of that death-bed scene. She recovered herself by an effort, and answered gently:

"It is past, Harry, my dear father is at rest; nothing can trouble him now. Your uncle's treatment of him has been one of the bitterest sorrows of my life; and, since his death, in the early days of my mourning, there have been times when the sight of old Mr. Clare would have been unbearable to me; and I should have shrunk from him with pain, almost with loathing. But, thank God, I have lived down such feelings! I can forgive him now, as freely as I hope to be forgiven. It is an evil thing to cherish the memory of an injury, it eats into the heart, and rankles there, a festering spot, that poisons all it touches."

"This is like you, my kind, patient Grace; but I cannot forget how deeply you have been wronged, for I have heard something of my uncle's cruel persecution. What passed in that interview, to which he alludes in that letter he sent to you at Woodlands—Tell me, only a few words, Grace. I will never again ask you to revive this painful subject, for I know that it opens old wounds."

It was thus that he led her on to talk of the past, to tell him all he was so tenderly anxious to learn. But she did so with a shrinking reluctance that he was not slow to understand. He knew it arose from her desire to spare him the pain o the knowledge; and rightly guessed, that with this motive, much of his uncle's harshness was generously concealed.

When she spoke of old Matthew's pecuniary claims upon her father, and the threats by which he had tried to enfore his own conditions of payment, it was then that Harry's agitation overcame his self-command, and he hastily interrupted: "Send your father to prison Grace, he could not! It was only to work upon your filial fears, but surely you did not bind yourself to such a pledge. You could not, if I still owned a place in your heart."

She looked at his pale agitated face, with a little shy reproach, and answered in a broken voice:—

"You were dear to me as ever, Harry, but I had the pen in my hand, ready to promise all your uncle wished, for my duty to my father seemed to leave me no other alternative. But he prevented me, forbade me in words I could not disobey. It was like a voice from the grave. His strength seemed restored to him by a miracle, but his life ebbed out in the effort. It was the excitement of that scene that hastened the end."

"And this was my uncle's doing," broke

out Harry, in violent emotion. "Oh! Grace, it was enough to make you hate the name of Clare, and all who bore it. To think that it was for this I consented to be exiled from all I loved, for this, I lived through a dreary time of torture, that I cannot now bear to look back upon, when the home sickness grew into a sort of maddening fever; when I thought of you incessantly, and pined for a few loving words from you, as a sick captive might pine for light and liberty. But, dearest, now we can let the past bury its troubled memories, and look only to the future, our future." He spoke with a softened intonation, and his face gathered a new light of love and tenderness, as he continued: "You will share it with me, Grace, and give me the right to shield your life from such cruel trials? You will be my wife?"

The soft brown eyes looked at him, through a mist of gathering tears, and the voice that answered him was low and faltering.

"Your uncle will never consent to our marriage, Harry. He has other views for you. He believes that he is securing your best interests. You would give up all, to keep your faith with me. It is kind, and noble, like yourself; but it will be selfish for me to suffer a sacrifice of your prospects. I, who have nothing to give in return."

"Hush! Grace, I will not hear this, it is treason to our love, and cruel injustice to your own heart. What could you give me, richer than your love, more precious than your own dear self? I ought to have told you that the decision no longer rests with my uncle, that his will docs not control mine. It is just that power should be forfeited, when it is abused."

She interrupted him, with a surprised start: "You do not mean that you have left your uncle, Harry?"

"Yes, Grace, I could not live on as I was, and retain my independence and self respect. There will be no sacrifice for me; I give up nothing. But you, Grace, ought I to wish you to link yourself with the chances of a poor man's lot? I cannot offer you luxuries, nor the home I have dreamed of for you; but I will do my best to make you happy. It is no vain self confidence to say that I do not fear the future if you share it with me. Darling, there will be some up-hill climbing, but with you by my side I feel that I could meet the world with a brave heart and willing hand. Say, will you trust me with your life's happiness?"

She was silent, but she crept nearer to him, and her little pale hand stole lovingly into his fervent clasp. This was more eloquent than words. He needed no other answer, for he felt that they were again re-united.

It was perhaps not a matter of surprise that the lovers should forget to take note of the passing time, but it could not be expected that Fanny Templeton in her self-imposed exile should be equally oblivious. It was the sound of her voice in the garden that suddenly recalled them to the world, which they had for the time forgotten in each other.

"Miss Templeton," exclaimed Harry gaily, "ah! that reminds me, Grace, I have a confession to make, for which I crave your forgiveness," and he poured into her wondering ear a recital of all his self-inflicted woes, his coldness to his old friend Cecil Lee, and the torture which he had suffered through his jealousy.

"I will not blame you, Harry," as I might have done," she answered gravely, "for the fault brought its own punishment; I have a shrewd guess that Mr. Lee would not feel particularly grateful for the hasty manner in which you disposed of his affections, which I am happy to know are much better engaged. Dear Fanny," she continued softly, as they caught a glimpse of the young heiress through the window, "what a treasure she will be to him."

Thus talking they passed into the garden,

Grace leaning on Harry's arm with a light in her eyes and a soft satisfied smile on her lips that told its own story.

Fanny read in one exulting glance all that she was longing to know, and rejoiced in the thought that she had had some influence in bringing about this happy state of things.

## CHAPTER XV.

A MONTH afterwards the little household at the sea-side was broken up, and the old tranquil life at Woodlands was resumed, with its quiet round of simple duties, interests and pleasures. Harry Clare went back to London, full of fresh spirit and energy, to work out the purpose which had given a new colour to his life, and stimulated by the thought that the happiness of a loving, true-hearted woman was dependent on his exertions. To make a home for Grace—this was his aim. She was pledged to him, heart and hand—no hostile influence could separate them now.

The soft, grey light of the autumn evening was fading calmly and pleasantly, like the close of a good life. Fanny Templeton and Grace sat together in the little parlour at Woodlands, enjoying a confidential chat, for Aunt Margaret was absent on a charitable visit to the cottage of one of her sick pensioners. There was a fire, for the evening was chill; but the lamp had not yet been lighted. The dim, fitful fire-light was in harmony with the quiet dreamy hour, and their talk flowed on with a gentle subdued ripple, that suited well the warmly toned atmosphere of the room.

"Now, Grace!" exclaimed Fanny, laughing demurely, "You will be obliged to acknowledge that I was right, when I defended your husband elect so warmly, on the morning you received that miserable, scurrilous letter from old Matthew Clare. I did not know him, but I was guided to my conviction by a certain instinct that never misleads me very far. I felt sure that he would prove himself a noble type of manhood, and a genuine fine fellow, that would make us all proud to know him. There, Grace, don't you think this speech of mine would give a twinge of jealousy to some one we know, who is foolish enough to mind a great deal about anything I say ?"

"No, dear Fanny, I do not, nor do you; we both believe *that* some one to be above such feelings; he would rather join in praise of a friend than seek to detract from it."

"Very charitably and profoundly argued, my most sage and conscientious Grace—you speak like an oracle. Who could imagine that you would ever allow yourself to talk such nonsense as you did this evening. You know I allude to the governess scheme; but I warn you that from this time it is a forbidden subject."

"But consider, dear Miss Templeton—"

"But consider, dear Miss Arnold," Fanny repeated, in playful mimicry, "no, I will not consider; the truth is, that I know already all you want to say, and decidedly negative all your arguments; for instance, this is the position of affairs. You and Mr. Clare have agreed that it will be wise to defer your marriage for a year, until he can establish himself, and see his way clear—very good. But in the mean time, you get certain crotchets in your head—saucy notions of independence, and acting upon them, you have the ungracious impertinence to tell me that you wish to take a situation as nursery governess. You are not satisfied with your experience of the slavery of the needle, but you wish to take out a new lease of bondage; to subject yourself to the whims and caprices of some selfish, narrow-minded, purse-proud woman, and her ill-regulated progeny of pampered pets. A nursery governess, indeed! It is little better than hiring yourself out as a machine, warranted to keep children's wardrobes in perfect order, dress their hair, and do every thing needful, with a certain amount of reading and spelling included in the account;

besides the getting up of mamma's frills and laces. I tell you, Grace Arnold, that you shall never be a nursery governess, if I can prevent it. It would be sin to suffer you to sacrifice a year of your life in such a manner."

"But, dear Fanny, you surely take an extreme view of the subject, and forgive me, love, I cannot help thinking that you are a little unjust to a class of—"

"It is no use pursuing the question, Grace," interrupted Fanny, hastily. "I will not argue the point, nor allow myself to be convinced by any of your logic. Let it suffice that you shall not be a nursery governess. There now we will dismiss the subject, for I am getting angry. Tell me, Grace, do you really want a change, are you tired of Woodlands?"

An arm was instantly thrown round her neck, and a pair of tearful, brown eyes, looked reproachfully into hers.

"Miss Templeton—Fanny, that was a cruel question. I did not deserve it, kind, generous lady; there is a bond between us, that nothing can ever break. It is the esteem and affection of a lifetime that can alone tell my grateful sense of all I owe you."

"Nonsense, Grace! you are making me sentimental. You owe me nothing, dear; the obligation is rather on my side, for you have done me good; association with you has drawn out the better part of my nature. It has been a quiet—almost insensibly correcting and elevating influence, and it has told upon my character, Grace. I shall be a better wife and a truer woman, through having lived with you. We cannot spare you, darling; you are becoming necessary to us, and we intend to keep you until Mr. Harry Clare has a husband's right to take you away. We shall recognise no other claim."

The arm of Grace was still wound lovingly round her neck; it needed no other answer than the assenting pressure of her hand, and one of her sweet, grave smiles to reassure Fanny. From that moment it was tacitly understood that the subject of the nursery governess was to be consigned to oblivion.

"By the by," commenced Fanny, gaily throwing off her serious manner, "I have news for your private ear, Grace; I have received a letter from my cousin, George Foster. You will remember, I told you of our ridiculous love passage. Poor fellow, he has got over his pique, and writes in a very proper spirit; now you need not look so grave, Grace. I am not going to make fun of my rejected knight, for I am determined to check that wicked propensity. But, seriously, I am sure he is improving, I always thought there was something to hope from him. You are aware that he and Harry Clare were school friends, and that it was from an accidental meeting with George in London, and some chance observation which he let fall concerning you, that Mr. Clare gained the clue to your retreat. Well, I find from my cousin's letter, that he has sought his friend's society, on every available opportunity; and the effect of such association, I am glad to see, is beginning to tell upon him. He is trying to correct his degenerate tastes and habits. It can be traced, even in his letter, for it is not so liberally sprinkled with sporting slang. He tells me that he has joined the army, I am glad to hear it, for I think that is just the profession to which he will best adapt himself, and in which he will be likely to find his element; and it will give him, what he needed, an occupation and a purpose in life. When he is once removed from the tyranny of his mother and sister, I predict that George will help to redeem the family credit. Stay, there is another important item of London news that I was positively forgetting, Grace. My cousin, Alice Foster, is going to be married in a few weeks. It has been announced in the fashionable world, with much preliminary puff; but I know nothing further than that it is considered a highly eligible match. Some French Count, I believe, whom they met at Brighton. Well, cousin Alice and I are not kindred spirits, but she has my good wishes; only, I hope that no young dress-maker will be victimised, in the making up of the wedding trousseau."

Fanny would have chatted on much longer, but for the interruption of the servant coming in to draw the curtains, and light the lamp; and the return of Aunt Margaret, almost immediately followed by the old doctor, who dropped in to spend the evening in his usual familiar way. He was accompanied, as a matter of course, by his nephew, Cecil, who still lingered at his uncle's, though the old gentleman had often laughingly ordered the idle dog to depart on his travels. But the young artist showed a suspicious reluctance to comply, and a very decided disposition to remain in the neighbourhood of Woodlands, haunting the shrine of his divinity.

° ° ° °

The year of probation was over, the year

of self-sacrifice, and brave, patient striving. Harry Clare had been successful, even beyond his most sanguine anticipations. It was not in vain that he had waited, hoped, and toiled, though his uncle's anger persecuted him with unrelenting vindictiveness, and baffled his efforts in many ways. But he was not to be discouraged, or turned aside; there was a strong-willed spirit of resistance in him, which when once roused, would not easily succumb to opposition. His was just the fearless, self-reliant character, that might be trusted to assert itself. A fortunate chance introduced him to the notice of a wealthy old merchant, a former friend and patron of his father's. This individual had long known and admired Harry Clare; he was acquainted with his skill in languages, and was not slow to discover the valuable business talents, which were thrown away in his present subordinate and irresponsible situation, and which he was shrewd enough to wish to turn to his own advantage. The result was, that the young man was engaged as his confidential clerk, and entrusted with the foreign correspondence of the extensive firm of which he was the head, at double the amount of salary which Harry Clare was then receiving, accompanied by a very intelligible hint of rapid advancement.

It was not long before the impatient lover began a series of mysterious visits to a certain pleasant suburb; if any friend had been sufficiently interested to take the trouble to watch his movements, they would have discovered —not exactly a "Rosamond's Bower," but something like it—a perfect gem of a house—half cottage, half villa, shrined in a sweet little garden—a sort of miniature Paradise, whose proportions were all on the most diminutive scale. This was Harry Clare's secret. It was here that all his leisure hours were spent. The cottage was a model of purity, freshness, and simple elegance—just the sort of home fitted for the reception of a young bride. It was easy to imagine that the neat little drawing room, with its sunny bay-window and soft, cloud-like muslin curtains, that gave it such a look of cool, airy grace, wanted only the crowning attraction of some fair, household face, and the charm of some gentle, womanly presence. This was the home prepared for dear Grace Arnold; here was the realization of the lover's dream.

° ° ° °

It was a memorable day at Woodlands. A day of joyous bustle and excitement, long to be remembered in the quiet, dreamy little village, which it roused to such unusual demonstration of interest and enthusiasm, for a double bridal was celebrated that morning. Fanny Templeton and Cecil Lee were united at the same time as Grace Arnold and Harry Clare.

A gay troop of the village school children, in their holiday attire, did honour to the occasion, spreading a fragrant carpet of flowers at the feet of the wedding party as they passed from the church to their carriages.

What could be more beautiful and appropriate than such offerings from childish hands? graceful tribute of earth's sweetest and fairest things, to young, loving, hopeful hearts, on the threshold of a new and untried life.

The poor were not forgotten in the festivities of the day, they rejoiced in an unlimited supply of good things. There was a generous treat provided for the school children, and at Woodlands in the evening there was a dinner and ball for the tenantry and servants.

It was in the midst of such rejoicings that the happy couples took their departure. The old doctor was in his element, as leader and master of the ceremonies. His parting benediction to his nephew was characteristic. He supposed the idle rogue would settle down and be content, now that he had succeeded in catching his sunbeam.

Dear Aunt Margaret was tranquilly happy, and found her element, as she always did, in dispensing happiness to others. She was assisted by George Foster, who remained at Woodlands an honoured and welcome guest.

The young officer fully justified his cousin's hopeful estimate of him. There was a decided change for the better. He had become graver and more thoughtful, which contributed much to the improvement of his conversation and manners. His regiment was then under orders for India, and he expressed himself with the enthusiasm of a true soldier, at the prospect of seeing some real service, and finding himself acting a part in the world.

* * * *

When the two brides took leave of each other after their wedding tour, while Fanny, divided between tears and smiles, was hanging tenderly on her friend's neck, she took occasion to thrust a sealed letter into the hand of Grace, which she imperatively commanded her not to open until she found herself snugly settled in that charming house, which she declared had almost made her out of love with dear, rambling old Woodlands.

Grace smilingly promised to obey, if curiosity did not tempt her too strongly, but she entirely forgot the little incident until a few days after, when the sight of Fanny's letter recalled it to her memory. But on opening it, to her astonishment and emotion, she discovered a bank cheque for One Thousand Pounds. The note contained these characteristic words, written in Fanny's well-known, dashing hand:

"Forgive my bit of stratagem, Mrs. Clare. It was forced upon me, for I knew that in no other way could I get your saucy, independent self to accept a present from me. I warn you and your husband, that often when not expected, I shall take it upon me to intrude upon the solitude of your dove's nest, for the purpose of taking lessons in matrimonial training. Don't chide me, dear, I can fancy how grave and serious you will be looking at all this light nonsense of mine. You see old habits of thought and speech are clinging to me still, and my matronly honours and dignities sit somewhat awkwardly upon me. But don't give me up in despair, Grace. I shall improve, and with your aid, learn how to discharge the duties of my new position. Farewell.

"Your ever devoted
"And attached,
"FANNY LEE.

"P.S.—A pretty short name, how do you like it in writing, dear? does it look as well as your own—Grace Clare? Yes, I am sure it does."

## CHAPTER XVI.

The end of five happy years found Harry Clare steadily working his way to prosperity. He was then one of the junior partners in the firm which he had entered as clerk, deservedly winning the esteem and confidence of those associated with him. He had not falsely estimated his capabilities. He was a self-made man in the truest and noblest sense of the term, for he had not elevated himself at the expense of others. He had never done violence to his conscience by heartless oppression of the fallen, nor taken ungenerous advantage of the unfortunate. His path to success had not been a selfish personal struggle, ruthlessly isolating him from the rest of humanity, and closing his heart against the kindly charities of life, to the exclusion of all other claims except those of self, and the sacrifice both of principle and feeling. Harry Clare was not one of this class of self-made men.

From the day of their marriage the most affectionate intimacy had been kept up between Grace and Fanny. The lady of Woodlands did not forget her threat about often intruding upon the solitude of the dove's nest, as she always called their cottage. She took particular delight in making short unceremonious visits at unexpected times, and inventing all kinds of pretexts to tempt Grace and her husband down to Woodlands.

Both households were gladdened by the presence of a little prattler. Harry Clare's was a son, a spirited noble boy, who had his mother's smile and deep brown eyes, and his father's clear frank brow. Cecil Lee's was a daughter, a lovely bright-eyed fairy, the idol and pet of every living thing about Woodlands. There was a pleasant little romance of match-making between the two young mothers. Fanny's vivid imagination had already decided that little Harry and her own pet Margaret were to love and marry each other.

This premature matrimonial scheme was a source of never failing interest and delight to one individual, whom it always excited to enthusiasm. This was Susan, who now held the important office of little Harry's nurse, and might be said to have attained the height of her simple ambition, for she still preserved all her old grateful admiring reverence for Grace and all that Grace loved. The kindly atmosphere of Woodlands, and the gentle government of Aunt Margaret, had worked a happy transformation in the little servant of the lodging house; she had now lost all personal identity with the poor over-worked drudge, who had so powerfully touched the womanly sympathies of Grace Arnold.

* * * *

The mild October day was fading slowly and sadly over the city. The dim lingering light and the soft sighing autumn wind had a strange mournfulness, that was more painfully felt in the dull cold streets with their busy self-engrossed crowds, and the presence of the hard facts of life. It reminded one of the dying leaves, and the slow solemn fading of the year; and seemed as if all things were touched with sorrowful regret for the bloom and beauty that was passing away.

Harry Clare must have been under the influence of such feelings that evening, for he was conscious of an unusual depression of spirit, for which he could not account to himself. Business had detained him at his office much beyond his accustomed hour. He was weary, both in body and mind, and might be forgiven for looking forward with such restless impatient longing to the happy home evening by his cosy fireside, with the dear home companionship, which always acted on his spirit like a soothing charm. With a sigh of relief he had just turned the key of his private desk, and was preparing to depart, when one of the clerks entered and handed to him a curious looking note, which he said had just been delivered by a boy, who was then waiting for an answer.

The young merchant hastily tore it open, and turned pale as he ran his eye over its contents. It was from his uncle's housekeeper, and contained only a few hurried blotted lines, which the agitation of the writer had made almost unreadable. It informed him that his uncle was dangerously ill, that the doctor gave no hopes of his recovery, and urged him for God's sake to come at once and see the old man before it was too late. This was a summons not likely to be coldly neglected by a man like Harry Clare, with his clear, high sense of duty, and his large, kindly human heart. He only delayed a few moments to write and despatch a hasty note to his wife, to relieve the painful uneasiness which he knew his protracted absence would occasion her.

There was something painful in re-visiting, under such circumstances, old Matthew Clare's gloomy home. To his nephew it looked more blighted and desolate than ever. Even the lean dog seemed to get leaner and fiercer as age grew upon him. Before going to the sick room, Harry paused to make some anxious inquiries about the invalid. He found himself again in the well-known parlour, which wore its old repelling look of comfortless rigid order. His uncle's vacant arm chair stood in its accustomed place, under the portrait of the hard-eyed old lady in the antique cap and gown—his grandmother Clare—to whose memory he was bound by no tender link of loving sympathy, for he remembered her as the unrelenting enemy of his kind-hearted gentle mother.

All that Harry's agitated questions could gain from the hurried answers of the half-bewildered housekeeper, only tended to confirm his worst fears about his uncle, and sent him to the sick room with a sad foreboding that the end was near, and a sorrowful, disappointed feeling that he owed his hasty summons more to the alarm and anxiety of the old servant, than, as he at first hoped, to the softening of his uncle's heart towards him.

It was a sad picture, that lonely, sick room, in the slowly gathering gloom of the dull October evening. The pale gleam of the shaded night lamp fell upon the stately, old-fashioned bed, on which the sufferer lay tossing in impatient, feverish restlessness, watched by no loving face, tended by no gentle ministering hand.

Harry Clare could not look unmoved at the old, hard face, which seemed to have grown so much older and harder since he last saw it. He could not look without a pitying yearning to be answered by one softened glance of kindly recognition. It touched him to think of the unblessed, loveless life thus waning to its close. To see the stricken old man, with all the hoarded riches for which he had toiled, sacrificed and sinned, powerless now, in his deepest need, to bind one human heart to him in genuine sympathy and love. To see him writhing in extreme physical pain, but with his iron will unbroken, and his proud spirit unsubdued, impotently rebelling against the helplessness of the body, yet clinging so tenaciously to its narrow prison!

How this aching void struck upon Harry Clare. How vividly he felt the absence of those religious consolations which can alone disarm Death of its sting.

The first sight of his nephew painfully excited the old man. His mouth contracted with a sudden convulsive spasm, and his eyelids quivered and fell, as he met the pitying, earnest eyes gazing at him so wistfully. But a momentary flash of the old, vindictive fire kindled in his restless grey eyes, as he made a vain effort to raise himself from his pillows, and something of the old passion trembled in his shaking voice, as his withered hands vehemently grasped the coverlet.

"You here, Harry Clare? I know you come to take your revenge, now I am helpless, powerless. You think the old man is going to die, and that you will be his heir.

Yes: it is the gold you want! you want it for your wife; the bankrupt's daughter; the proud, pale-faced thing that has come between me and all my heart's desires. But I will not die! I will live to guard my wealth, and disappoint you all."

His voice sank to a hoarse whisper: he ceased from pure exhaustion.

Harry shuddered at the bitter, wrathful words, and the insight they gave him into the darkened soul, so utterly unprepared for the dread coming change.

"You wrong, me, uncle, as God is my judge, in this solemn hour; I am here with no other motive than to serve you, as it is my duty; to try to be to you all you need in your extremity, and to assure you that the past is forgotten and forgiven, so far as it concerns me and mine."

There was irresistible pathos and power in every word that fell upon the hush of the sick room, strongly contrasting with the old man's impotent trembling passion. No self-serving purpose was in the soul that spoke out there, no insincerity in that low, earnest voice; it was the true, natural language of one who had knelt in spirit at the feet of the great Teacher, and taken to heart the simple, grand morality of His Gospel lessons.

A strange, questioning, troubled look crept over the face of Old Matthew Clare. Did his nephew's words bring round him an accusing host of memories? Was he stánding once more by that forlorn bed in the miserable lodging-house chamber, confronting again the soft, pleading eyes of that tall, slight girl, pale and worn with toil and watching, yet so powerful in her endurance and filial love; strong, even in her weakness, as she stood between him and her dying father, vainly striving to guard him from the insulting taunts of his remorseless visitor? Or was he thinking of the letters from India, which he had so pitilessly sacrificed? Was there no remorseful sting in the memory of that treacherous breach of trust, which he would never have forgiven in another? But whatever might be the conflicting thoughts and feelings which agitated him in that hour, he gave no outward sign.

His failing, vital powers seemed to have been spent in the first burst of excitement. He lay pale and gasping for breath, vainly struggling to speak, but unable to make himself understood. He seemed to fear that his nephew would leave him, for he caught his hand and grasped it with a force for which he seemed to have collected the last remains of physical strength. When the doctor saw his patient, he pronounced him much worse, and imperatively forbade the introduction of any subject that might tend to renew excitement, which might be fatal. Harry faithfully watched by the sick bed through the long, weary night, which was but a type of others that succeeded.

Before the end of the week the physician's worst fears were realised. The old man sank rapidly; but the passions which had governed him through life, still retained their ascendancy, and reigned supreme, even in that dread hour, when it became evident to all around him, that the tide of life was ebbing away—and the rebellious, tortured spirit clung with redoubled tenacity to the world, which was fading from it. As long as he could speak, the sick man broke out at intervals into wild, frightened appeals to the doctor and his nephew.

"It's false! I'm not going to die! It's only a trick to frighten me; but it's no use—my will is safe—it cannot be that I shall die now, with all my money! Oh, doctor! tell me there is hope!"

It was a very painful death-bed, and left an impression on the mind of the sensitive Harry Clare, which time never effaced.

It was only once, towards the last, that his uncle softened towards him. He motioned him to come nearer, and bending down, Harry made out with much difficulty, the slow, broken words:—

"Forgotten and forgiven, did you say?

Harry—nephew—I always liked you more than—any one—in—the—world—except—except—your—father; and—I built—all my—hopes—in you."

Here there was a pause, which Harry did not venture to break. His uncle went on slowly and painfully: "You have a boy, called—after you—Harry—Clare—take care—of him,—though he—is—her son—he shall have—my blessing—and—and—something—else; remember—I—I could—not rest—if my—money—did not—go—to a—a—Clare."

Those were nearly his last words. He gradually sank into a state of unconsciousness, which was but a foreshadowing of the end. On the peaceful Sunday morning, when the holy sabbath hush was over the toil-wearied city, and the church bells were ringing out their sweet, solemn invitations to God's temple—the rich man died.

There was a little excited gossip among Matthew Clare's friends in the city, as to how the miserly old man had disposed of his money. But the general curiosity, on this doubtful point, was satisfied by Harry's presence at the funeral; and the fact that the uncle and nephew had been reconciled to each other. So on the presumption of his anticipated good fortune, Harry Clare—in the novel character of a great capitalist—found himself suddenly exalted into a personage of no slight importance; courted by needy traders, with a view to his future patronage, and surrounded by hosts of new friends, who seemed anxious to devote their lives to his service.

There was deeper meaning than Harry Clare suspected, in the old man's dying words about his boy. They were forcibly recalled to him on the reading of the will; when, much to his surprise, he found, that, with the exception of a few trifling legacies, his uncle had bequeathed the whole of his property without reserve to his little son, Harry; subject to his guardianship, conjointly with a trusted business friend of his uncle's, who was named co-executor.

## CHAPTER XVII.

When first informed of the unexpected inheritance which had fallen to the lot of her darling boy, Grace thoughtfully drew the child towards her, and a tear fell on the wondering little face, as she softly kissed him. Her look was full of grave earnestness, as she whispered to her husband:

"Harry, this wealth will be a great responsibility. It must be our care that it proves good for our boy. We must teach him that wealth is to be valued, not for itself, but for the good that it enables us to do; and that it can only become a blessing by being used as the means to work out good, unselfish aims. Dear husband, I should regret this fortune, if I thought that its influence would make our darling less like you, or deprive him of that noble spirit of self-dependence, which to you has proved better than riches."

° ° ° °

On carefully examining the contents of a small pocket book, which his uncle had placed in his hands, a few hours before his death, Harry found a note, addressed to himself, which had before escaped his notice; by its date, and the wavering, almost illegible, handwriting, he judged that it had been written during the old man's last illness. It contained these words:

"As you are now aware that certain letters from India never reached the person to whom they were addressed, I think it right to tell you, that they were destroyed on the night that you and I first clearly understood our respective views and intentions. I do not extenuate the act, nor do I make excuses for it. I know that it was a breach of honour; but I should repeat it under similar provocation. As it is, I regret that it was so utterly powerless to secure my object, which was to prevent your marriage. If you desire revenge, it will please you to know, that whatever I have made you suffer, has been paid back to me with interest; for you have turned my last years to bitterness, and stung me through the loss of all that I had set my heart upon."

* * * *

Harry Clare was deeply grieved as he read this painful record of the blind, misguided passions, whose consuming fire had only been quenched in death; and grieved also to see that the hatred to his sweet wife was still unrelenting as of old.

* * * *

It was a few months after the death of old Matthew Clare, that the quiet circle at Woodlands were startled by a fragment of fashionable town gossip, which had already created no little sensation in some polite circles, where it had been pretty freely discussed by certain fair friends of the lady. The report was, that Alice Foster's brilliant marriage had proved a mere bubble, which had suddenly burst in shame and humiliation. That her husband, the vaunted French Count, was discovered to be nothing better than an unprincipled gambling adventurer, who had assumed a false character for the purpose of entrapping a fortune. It was added that the deceived, indignant wife had returned to her father's house, where her presence at that time would be regarded as an additional misfortune, for it was known that Mr. Foster's affairs were so seriously embarrassed as to necessitate some very mortifying retrenchment in the family expenditure. There were hints that the fashionable London mansion was about to be given up, and that the family were going to retire into the country for a time. Mr. Foster's broken health and the unhappiness of poor Alice were made the pretexts for these changes. But none of Mrs. Foster's *dear* friends were deceived—they all knew the real state of affairs. The truth of these rumours was soon confirmed at Woodlands, by an unexpected letter from Mrs. Foster—a long, exculpatory epistle, humble, supplicating—almost servile in its tone of self-abasement, in which the writer dilated upon her domestic misfortunes, not the least of which, she artfully affirmed, was the lamentable breach now existing between herself and her dearly loved niece.

This letter pained Fanny. She had no sympathy with meanness or cowardice in any form, and frankly confessed that she could have more respect for Aunt Foster, even in her original character—unamiable and faulty as it was, for this sudden attempt at conciliation, with so much over-strained, unnatural humility was not an improvement on her old manner.

But the kind hearts at Woodlands did not

neglect Mrs. Foster's appeal. It was responded to by such substantial proofs of sympathy as that lady was most likely to appreciate. Poor Mrs. Foster! even her enemies might pity her in this time of bitter mortification and reverse. The pecuniary embarrassments were every day becoming more serious; and now her danghter, embittered in temper, and utterly engrossed with herself and her own wrongs, was returned upon her hands, to be a daily source of torture and reproach.

Mr. Foster, a hopelessly confirmed invalid —discord and disunion among her sons; and George, the only one from whom she could expect consolation, absent with his regiment on foreign service! All this made an accumulated burthen of family troubles, peculiarly distressing to one with Mrs. Foster's organization and habits, and one which she had neither mental strength nor moral courage to meet.

We have little more to add before we close our quiet history. Only this—that it would be difficult to find, in all the wide world, two happier homes than those of Woodlands and the Dove's Nest. Grace and Harry still lived in the pleasant little cottage to which Fanny had given that name; though their worldly prospects would then have warranted its exchange for a more ambitious residence, and many of their acquaintances often expressed their wonder that the Clares did not keep up a little more becoming style. But Grace could not be prevailed upon to leave the bright little bridal home which such loving care and labour had prepared for her, and to which she was bound by so many tender associations.

Dear, gentle Grace! It was not her ambition to be called a model woman—to shine as a guiding light before the world, or take her place among the teachers and leaders of the age. She chose to keep stedfastly to her own quiet path of duty, striving to do her woman's work wisely and well, with the unsuspected strength of will, the quiet tenacity of purpose, and the sweet, thoughtful earnestness which had been always characteristic of her ; content in her simple sphere of usefulness, and craving to be nothing more than a good household spirit—loving, and being loved; coveting no wider empire than the hearts in which she reigned; and no higher destiny than to fulfil the beautiful woman's mission of a true wife and mother.

Heaven send us more of these noble, simple, unobtrusive spirits! We need to have such pure, gentle lives woven like golden threads through the future history of the world.

We need them and their influence, for such homes are the great centres of a nation's civilisation; and such wives and mothers are the true guarantee for the future greatness of its people.

THE END.

CPSIA information can be obtained
at www.ICGtesting.com
Printed in the USA
LVHW100440110522
718424LV00003B/177

9 783375 003371